PIRATE'S CURSE

THE BERKANO VAMPIRE COLLECTION – DIVISION 1

LEIGH ANDERSON

REBECCA HAMILTON

FALLEN SORCERY

COPYRIGHT

DESCRIPTION

Once upon a time, a vampire and a witch fell in love, and that love fractured the world. Now divided into sixteen isolated Divisions, the world is an unstable and dangerous place.

In the Division of NOLA, Catheryn Beauregard fears her burgeoning magical powers. Hiding as just another slave in the home of the Hoodoo Queen, Catheryn hopes her simplistic powers will go unnoticed. And her plan seems to be working...until the Hoodoo House is attacked by a ruthless band of vampire pirates.

Captain Rainier Dulocke and his crew need humans to feed on. In an act of desperation, they beset the Hoodoo House and take ten slaves to sustain them. Rainier takes a girl named Catheryn for himself, but her blood is giving him terrible side effects. Still, he refuses to give her up. Even when the Hoodoo Queen demands her return.

The NOLA Division is in danger. The waters are rising. Food is running out. And the Hoodoo Queen is about to destroy everything that's left if the pirates don't meet her request. Now Catheryn must choose who will die: the humans who sold her, the witches who bought her, or vampires who stole her. If she fails to decide, everyone could die.

CHAPTER 1

Don't *breathe*, Catheryn thought. *If you breathe, you're dead.*

From her place in the closet, she could see the flicker of torchlight as the pirates ran back and forth through the house. The *vampire* pirates. The most dangerous creatures she knew of. They needed human blood to live. *Her* blood. The blood of her fellow slaves. But what were they doing here? In the Hoodoo House? She was supposed to be safe here. The Hoodoo Queen was a powerful woman. Surely she could fight them off. All Catheryn had to do was be quiet. Be still. *Don't breathe.*

Catheryn clenched and flexed her fingers. There were no weapons in the closet. If someone found her, she would have no way to defend herself. She looked at her hands and willed them to do…something. Anything.

This closet was her safe place. A small nook under the stairs she often visited when she wanted to be alone, to collect her thoughts. To practice her budding magic. She had already been hiding in the closet before the pirates arrived. Though this time, she hadn't been planning on coming out.

Because this time, she hadn't hidden away to work on her

magic. She'd hidden because she'd screwed up. One of the other witches had caught her. There had been a struggle. The knife...

Catheryn held her hand over her mouth. She had fled to the closet, unsure of what to do. She had been afraid of what would happen to her once the Hoodoo Queen found out what she had done. Now, her fear of the pirates far surpassed her fear of the queen. The queen might simply punish her. Maybe sell her to another owner. But the pirates? They would kill her. They would suck her blood until her heart stilled.

Come on, she said to herself as she held her hands in front of her. *Work!*

She had no idea just what kind of magic she possessed, if she was even a real witch or not. She always thought she was a normal human. Until she realized that sometimes things just...happened. A spark here, a chair inching to the side there. Did she really have any magic powers at all? Or was it all in her head? Was some of the magic from the witches in the Hoodoo House rubbing off on her? Was it all just a coincidence? She didn't know. But as the sounds of screams and fighting grew stronger and louder, for the first time she hoped she would have some way to fight back if she were discovered. Some inkling of magic. Or even full-blown magic powers. Only the witches would survive this night, she was sure.

"Hey! Check over there!" barked one of the pirates.

Her breath hitched in her throat, and she stepped deeper into the closet, pressing herself firmly against the back wall. Through the slats in the door, the orange torchlight burned brightly. They were close.

A shadow moved past. He was going to find her.

"*Save me!*" she whispered to herself.

The pirate opened the door. "Got ya!"

Catheryn shrieked as a panel she didn't know existed opened behind her and she fell. She screamed as she fell down the hole, holding her arms around her head to protect it. Her elbows and knees banged painfully against the walls of the narrow tunnel, and she landed with a thud on the wooden floor so hard it knocked the wind out of her.

"What's this?" asked a male voice. "Dinner from above?"

Several voices laughed.

She opened her eyes, her heart pounding in her chest. She was lying in front of booted feet. Slowly, she lifted her gaze, taking in a man who towered over her. He wore the dark blue and gold threaded coat of a naval officer, which was most certainly stolen. His hand rested on the hilt of a large cutlass, still in its scabbard.

This man was not concerned about the battle raging around him. He held himself with surety that his men would do the job he had set them to. His shirt fell slightly open, revealing a broad chest. She dared to look at his face, which she would almost consider handsome had she not been in fear for her life. He was clean-shaven with long hair tied loosely behind him. He was Caucasian, which was a rarity for this part of the world, though all vampires—no matter their race—had an unnatural paleness to them.

Naturally, he'd topped his head with a large tricorn hat. Most pirates were as obsessed with the fanciful pirate tales of old, no matter how inaccurate, as everyone else was back before the Rift...from before the world was ripped asunder.

"She sure looks yummy, cap'n," one of the other men said.

To her side, a truly odiferous man with scraggly hair and missing and crooked teeth practically slobbered over the idea of sucking her blood.

"Take her away, Mathis," the captain said, waving his hand dismissively. "Put her with the others."

She stood quickly as the man named Mathis lunged toward her.

"Stop!" she yelled, holding her hand flat in front of her.

For a moment—the briefest moment—she thought he froze. Or maybe it was simply the flight mode she felt herself in, because she turned and darted away so quickly the captain the other pirates around her did not have time to react. She slipped past them, up the stairs, and out the back door. Once at the top, she paused, glancing back to the house and out to woods beyond. She could run for her life...but no. She ground her teeth together and tamped down the urge to flee. She had to help the others.

She darted through the yard, weaving around witches fighting with pirates, either party too busy with one another to concern themselves with her. Fire and lightning shot from the witches' hands as the pirates slashed at them with swords and shot them with guns.

Usually witches would have the upper hand against vampires. Magic was more powerful than mundane weapons, after all. But there were *so many* pirates. More than Catheryn had ever seen. Enough so that the witches struggled to hold the pirates back.

But Catheryn couldn't think about that. She had to help the other humans—the slaves like her. The closest thing she had to family, and who the pirates had surely come here to pillage.

Unfortunately for humans, vampires could only survive on human blood. Witch blood was deadly to them. And unfortunately for her, The Hoodoo Queen she lived with owned a stable of human slaves. *That* was why the vampires were here. If Catheryn could help the humans escape, they would be safe, and the vampires would leave.

But as Catheryn approached the slave quarters, she realized she was too late. Vampires already surrounded it. Of course... That is the first place the vampires would have gone.

Some of the vampires had already given into their cravings and were feeding on the slaves. Some of the slaves were already dead or dying. As much as Catheryn wanted to help, she was no hero. They were beyond her saving. She needed to find the other slaves—the ones who still had a chance.

Sneaking around the back of the slave quarters, she slipped

inside the quarters through a small opening between some of the boards.

"Catheryn!" gasped one of the slaves. An older woman. "What are you doing here, child? You need to get away!"

"The house is surrounded," Catheryn said. "I fear the Hoodoo Queen isn't going to be able to hold them back. We need to escape."

"How?" another slave asked. "I can't fit through there. And where will we go if the pirates have us surrounded?"

"We're going to be killed!"

"What are we going to do?"

The slaves were in a panic. She probably shouldn't have said so much so soon. But they were right. Where *would* they go? And if the vampires didn't find them and drain them, they would just be recaptured by the Hoodoo Queen and dragged back to slavery anyway. What was the point?

Not dying. Not dying is the point.

Right, she told herself. They needed to at least *try*. She was a survivor. She had to be—at least until she found her sister. Eva could still be out there, somewhere. So Catheryn had to survive, even if only for her. So that someday they might find one another again.

Catheryn walked to the front of the slave quarters where several people were guarding the door, trying to keep the vampires from breaking in. Raising her hands, she chanted, "Protect us!"

Nothing happened.

"What are you doing, Catheryn, you daft girl?" asked one of the men holding the door closed.

Catheryn tried again. "Help us!"

Again, nothing happened.

"Catheryn!" another slave called to her. "Help *me!* Come bar the door."

Catheryn looked around for something that could help. She grabbed a chair and ran over to brace the door.

But it didn't work.

With a large *boom,* the door splintered open, and the people closest to it were sent flying backward, including Catheryn. The pirates must have used an explosive device to break through. A man next to her screamed as he clawed at a large piece of wood sticking out of his eye. A woman to her right lay dead, a shard of wood sticking out of her chest like a stake.

Like a stake!

Catheryn's brain was in a daze, and everything seemed to be moving in slow motion, but that thought shot her into motion. She touched her head, her chest, and realized that she was uninjured. She shook herself out of her dizziness and reached for the chair she had been holding earlier. It had been smashed into many pieces, so she grabbed a loose chair leg and stood, brandishing it like a bat.

As the smoke cleared, the man she had seen earlier—the vampire pirate captain—stepped forward.

"Round them up!" he said.

The other slaves screamed, running to escape as the pirates descended on them like a plague of locusts.

Catheryn's heart raced, but she steeled herself as she stepped forward.

"You'll not hurt them!" she called out.

Of course, she could not stop him, and he would probably kill her. But if she could distract him, even for a moment, maybe some of the other slaves could escape.

The pirate captain locked eyes with her. "There you are," he said. "I was wondering where you ran off to."

Mathis stepped toward her, but the captain stopped him.

"No," he said. "She's mine."

Mathis shrugged and turned his attention on another hapless girl who was trying to escape. But Catheryn couldn't focus on her right now. Vampires were fast—notoriously fast. She couldn't take her eyes off of the captain for even a moment if she hoped to survive.

Who was she kidding? She wasn't going to survive this. He was a vampire. A pirate. A skilled fighter and a bloodthirsty monster. She was going to die.

At least she would go down fighting.

The pirate assumed a proper swordsman's stance, and Catheryn stepped forward. Her foot brushed against something, and she reached down without taking her eyes off the pirate to pick it up. It was another piece of wood. She held it and the chair leg in front of her like a cross.

"Be gone, demon!" she yelled.

The pirate smirked. "Oh my. Whatever will I do?"

His smirk turned into a hearty laugh as he stepped forward quickly, so quickly it was if he had transported several feet closer to her. He flicked his sword and knocked the piece of wood out of her hand.

Now standing before him with only the chair leg for protection, she turned to the side, mimicking the way the pirate stood, and held the chair leg like a sword. It was too heavy and awkward to hold in such a manner, much less to be wielded effectively, but at least she was doing something.

The pirate advanced on her and slashed with his sword. She held up the chair leg to block him, but the impact of metal against thick wood reverberated through her. He hacked at her again, and again. Each time, she held the chair leg up, but she was forced to step back to keep from losing her balance and falling. He would soon hack through her only weapon, and then she would be dead.

He raised his sword with a smile on his face. He was toying with her. He could have disarmed her easily, but he was enjoying the fight, like a cat playing with a mouse before the prey became a meal. He mustn't have thought Catheryn actually posed a threat to him. Could she use that to her advantage?

As he lunged toward her one last time, she yelled, "Freeze!"

And he did, for just a moment. Just long enough for her to spin out of his path and whack his arm with the chair leg.

The pirate groaned and dropped his sword. He looked at her and glared. She wacked him with the chair leg again, right on his shoulder. He again yelled out, his face contorting with pain.

The other humans saw what was happening, that Catheryn was actually beating the pirate captain with a stick, and it seemed to bolster them. All at once, they turned on their pirate tormentors. The pirates seemed stunned that the humans would dare defy them.

Catheryn felt herself smile as she raised her chair leg to hit the captain again, but she had let down her guard. Her moment of confidence had cost her the upper hand. As she swung, he reached up with his other arm and grabbed the chair leg firmly. He ripped it from her hands and threw it aside. Catheryn took a step back, but the pirate grabbed her around the throat.

"I am going to make sure you live to regret that," he said with a growl.

He opened his mouth, baring his sharp, cruel fangs. He was going to bite her—was going to *eat* her—right here and now. This was it.

I'm sorry, Eva, she thought to herself.

Catheryn tried to fight back. She struggled in his arms and screamed for help.

"Stop! Stop! Freeze!" she yelled in a panic, but nothing happened, and no one could come to her aid.

"Captain!" someone called out. One of his men running toward him. "Captain, we found her! Come quick! She's trapped!"

The captain smiled and turned back to the rest of his men who were still chasing and abusing the slaves in the yard. "Round them up and bring them inside!" he yelled. Then he turned back to Catheryn. "You're coming with me, troublemaker."

Then Catheryn felt a sharp pain in the side of her head. She didn't pass out, but she stumbled, and her vision blurred out of focus, leaving her with no choice but to let the vampire drag her back toward the Hoodoo House.

Whatever he planned to do, she was not sure, but likely, she would wish she hadn't lived to see it.

CHAPTER 2

Earlier that day...

Captain Rainier watched as his first mate Mathis kicked the last dried up husk of a former human being over the side of the ship.

"That's the last of our food supply, captain," Mathis said. "We have no choice but to go on a raid."

The captain clenched his teeth and blew a thin breath between them. "What's the nearest port?" he asked, but he already knew the unwanted answer.

"NOLA," the mate said. "Under witch control."

"The second nearest port, then?" Rainier asked.

"Too far," the mate replied. "The men will be starving by then. Some of them already are. The most feral I've already clapped in irons below deck, but their numbers will only grow."

Rainier grumbled to himself. He knew it was true, but sailing right into witch territory was about the worst scenario he could think of.

"It will be high tide just before dusk," Rainier said. "How high is the tide now?"

"Pretty damn high, sir," Mathis said. "Reports say the waters have risen so high in NOLA you can practically sail right up to the front door of the Hoodoo House."

Rainer turned to the ship's medic. "How many men are in fighting form?"

"I'd say about a hundred and fifty."

"There are only about fifty witches in the Hoodoo House coven, correct?" the captain asked no one in particular.

"Aye," Mathis said. "But fifty of the most powerful witches in NOLA, or any Division for that matter. It would be a fierce battle."

"Can't eat witches, sir," one of the other pirates piped up.

"I know that, you fool," the captain said with more calm than the idiot deserved. "But the witches of NOLA keep humans as slaves. The Hoodoo House is said to have a rather large passel of them. She uses them for labor and to trade as goods."

The first mate nodded, standing at attention. "What are your orders, captain?"

Rainier sighed. He would certainly lose some men, but far fewer than if they stayed out to sea and starved.

"Rally the men," he said. "We attack the Hoodoo House at dusk."

As the woman sprawled at his feet looked up at him, it was as if someone had struck him. He was captivated by her. Her eyes were deep and dark, and he wanted nothing more than to swim in them. Her lovely face was framed with curling black hair. As he took in her whole face, though, he realized her gaze was not one of equal admiration, but of fear.

As it should be, he thought, clearing his throat and refocusing on the task at hand.

He was ransacking the house looking for women and men like

her to take back to the ship and feast upon. He shook his head and recalled his purpose.

"Put her with the others," he ordered. But the woman fought back. She was quick and nimble, and his worthless deckhands let her slip away.

"Find her, you mangy dogs!" he ordered.

Captain Rainier marched through the house, fighting powerful witches and desperate humans along the way. He, being a vampire, did not possess magic the way the witches did, but he was strong and fast. He needed to find the Hoodoo Queen. If he could take her down, the whole house would fall. But she would not be easy prey.

His men seemed to be gaining the upper hand against the witches. Their surprise attack and sheer numbers overwhelmed the witches, just as he had planned. He made his way to the slave barracks behind the house. He needed to find the humans and drag them back to the ship. Even if he didn't defeat the Hoodoo Queen, if he could just grab the booty, that would be enough.

The human chattel had barricaded themselves inside their quarters, which was not much more than a shed in the backyard of the house. Some of the men circled the barracks with torches, planning to smoke the humans out. Rainier ordered them to fall back. He couldn't risk the humans dying; they couldn't eat dead blood. And even if they just used smoke and didn't burn the barracks down, the humans might still refuse to come out. Most humans would rather die of smoke inhalation than as a vampire's dinner.

He motioned for a man with a torch to come near. He reached to his belt and pulled out a small grenade, then lit the fuse with the torch and rolled it toward the door of the barracks.

The door exploded, sending several pirates and humans flying. A couple of the humans had been killed in the explosion, but there were still plenty more—more than he expected. Dozens of humans poured out of the barracks screaming.

But one human approached him with a steady gaze. The woman who had dropped from the sky at his feet.

"There you are," he said. "I was wondering where you ran off to."

He had to admire the woman's spunk. He was stronger, faster, and deadlier than this girl. Yet here she stood, brandishing a silly chair leg as if she stood a chance. It would be almost comical if she wasn't fighting for her life.

She then picked up a piece of wood from the shattered door and held it and the chair leg like a cross in front of her. He smirked. So many humans still believed such silly nonsense about vampires. Oh well. The vampires encouraged such misinformation. It often gave them the upper hand in a battle, like right now.

He disarmed her left hand of the shard of wood and could have disarmed her of the chair leg in her right hand as well...but he was enjoying the game. The smell of fear that pulsed through her veins was intoxicating. He licked his lips as he stepped forward and slashed at her chair leg. She blocked his attack, and he struck again. Again she deflected. Had she been a vampire, he could have trained her to be a very good pirate. But he had no more time for this. He needed to round up the bloodbags and go.

Time to stop playing around. He would take this woman for himself. As the captain, he could have his own blood slave and wouldn't have to share her. He lunged for her, ready to disarm her and end the farce.

"Freeze!" she yelled.

The sudden surge of strength in her voice, even though she was clearly losing the fight, gave him pause. He should have known better. *Never let your guard down,* he chided himself. He could hardly believe it when she managed to get a whack in on his arm. He actually cried out in pain and dropped his sword. Him! The fiercest vampire pirate captain of the dark seas! He turned just as she whacked him again, this time across the shoulder.

Oh, how she would pay.

He mustered his strength, and as she reeled back, getting ready to strike again, he turned and grabbed the chair leg with one hand and her neck with the other. She dropped the chair leg, and her eyes went wide, the pheromones of fear rolling off of her in tantalizing waves.

"I am going to make sure you live to regret that," he said with a growl.

As he pulled her close, the woman screamed and struggled in his grasp. He opened his mouth. Just a quick drink would subdue her until he got her to the ship. He was just about to bite when one of his men called out.

"Captain, we found her! Come quick! She's trapped!"

He smiled and looked at the men who were working on collecting and tying up the humans they had been able to capture so far. "Round them up and bring them inside!" he yelled. Then he turned back to the girl. "You're coming with me, troublemaker."

He took his backhand to the side of her head. He didn't hit her hard enough to knock her out, but she stumbled. He motioned for one of the men to drag her into the house, along with the rest of the booty.

Captain Rainier followed his men back inside the Hoodoo House. The house was huge, with many floors, rooms, and winding passages. He suspected the house itself was enchanted, and a person could get lost inside of it forever if they weren't careful.

He finally came to a large room. On one side stood the witches, led by the Hoodoo Queen. On the other were the vampires, just waiting on the signal from Rainier to attack. The queen was protecting not just her fellow witches, but many of her human property as well. The pirates were licking their chops just staring at the delicious mortals.

"Your Majesty," Rainier said in a mocking tone with an exaggerated bow. "It has been a long time."

"Not long enough," she said. The queen stood defiant. Her skin was dark as night but painted with sacred symbols in green and yellow. Her hair was pulled back from her face but hung in long tendrils around her shoulders, undisturbed aside from the large black crow sitting on one side.

"You have been defeated," Rainier stated. "Give us what we need and we will let you live."

"I have not been defeated yet," she said. When she moved, her layered clothes jingled with bells. "You think I don't still have a few tricks up my sleeve?"

The Hoodoo Queen then raised her arms, and the whole house groaned and shook. The pirates murmured and back away.

"You would bring your whole house down on us?" Rainier asked. "You would die, too."

"It would be worth it," she said, "to rid what little we have left of the world of the likes of you."

Rainier was much faster than she was. He could zip across the room and slice through her neck in the blink of an eye. But he couldn't take out the others. If he was focused only on the queen, one of the others could take him out. She also might have the house booby-trapped. She could have it protected with a spell that would destroy it if she died. But he couldn't leave without food. He could let the queen live and take out more of her acolytes, weaken her further. But that would give her the upper hand to attack him. There really were no good options here.

Without the need to speak, both Captain Rainier and the Hoodoo Queen knew they were at an impasse.

"We are civilized people," Rainier said. "Surely we can come to some sort of arrangement."

"Like what?" the queen asked.

"You know what we need," he said.

She arched her eyebrow. "Do I?"

"We need blood. We need a supply of food to take with us."

"These humans are *my* property," she said. "I also have need of them."

"I'm not asking for all of them," he said. "Just enough to tide us over until we can move on to a...more desirable hunting location."

The queen stood quiet. One of the witches standing near her squeezed her arm, as if to tell her not to trust the vampires. The humans who had run to the queen's side also began to fidget as they suddenly began to doubt her ability, or willingness, to save them.

"I will give you five humans," she finally said. Several of the humans around her gasped and began to beg her not to do this, she she silenced them with a quick movement of her arm and a sharp hush.

"I have a ship of hundreds of men," Rainier said. "I would need at least twenty slaves."

"How many did you already kill?" the queen asked through gritted teeth. "I can feel the heartbeat of every person, witch or human, who lives in my city. Do you know how many stilled this night?"

Rainier was silent. He had no idea how many had been killed or fed from during the fighting.

"You will take ten humans," she said. "And not one more."

Rainier nodded. "It is acceptable." He turned to his men. "See how many the other men have already captured, then..."

"But," the Hoodoo Queen interrupted. Rainier turned back to her. "If you ever return to the Hoodoo House, if you ever step foot again in NOLA, I *will* kill you, and all of your men. You know I can do this."

Rainier nodded. He couldn't really promise he would never return to NOLA. It was a valuable trade port. But he would give the queen his word...for now.

"It is agreed," Rainier said with a sharp bow. He then turned to

Mathis. "See how many slaves the men have already rounded up. Choose nine slaves for sharing."

"Nine?" Mathis asked. "But she said..."

"I know what she said," he replied. "As captain, I will take one as my personal devotee."

He looked around the room for one woman in particular. The one who had dared to fight him earlier. The one with dark eyes and the fighting spirit.

He saw her, on the floor, pressed up against the wall. Their eyes met, and a surge of electricity coursed through him. It was as if nothing else mattered and no one else was present. He wanted this woman, needed her. And soon, he would possess her.

"This one," he said, pointing to the woman. "This one is mine."

C atheryn's breath hitched in her throat. "How could you?" she asked accusingly of the Hoodoo Queen. Catheryn scrambled to her feet and approached the queen. "We trusted you. Believed in you!"

"Step back, child," the queen said. "This is just business. Nothing personal."

"Nothing personal?" Catheryn demanded. "This...this is my *life* we are talking about. It doesn't *get* any more personal than that! You know this is a death sentence! Vampires are monsters. They can only survive by drinking us dry!"

"That is enough, girl," the captain said, gripping her arm and turning him to her. "I'll take good care of you."

"Until you don't," Catheryn spat.

She'd thought she would be safe here, hidden among the throng of humans who served the Hoodoo Queen. The queen was supposedly the most powerful woman in NOLA, yet she couldn't even defend her own property?

Maybe this was magic at work, Catheryn thought. A sort of karma for what she did earlier, before the pirates attacked. The real reason she had been hiding in the hovel under the stairs. This was her punishment.

Or was it her redemption? If the Hoodoo Queen found out what Catheryn had done, her vengeance would be wrathful indeed. Maybe this was her saving grace. If the pirate took her away, maybe Catheryn could escape. She could escape from both the vampires and the witches. She just needed a plan...

Unfortunately, she didn't have one. At least not yet.

The pirate captain pulled at her arm, trying to drag her away, and she looked him full in the face. There was a hunger in his eyes. A hunger that made Catheryn recoil in fear.

Typically, a vampire could subsist on a single human for weeks, or even months. If a vampire drank from his devotee in moderation, and allowed the human's natural supply of blood to replenish, the human could survive several feedings.

But most vampires didn't practice moderation. Especially if they were already starving when they found their prey. Catheryn feared for the humans who were going to be shared by the rest of the ship's crew. How could they survive even one night of feeding hundreds of hungry pirates?

No, Catheryn doubted she would survive long enough to escape if she willingly went with the pirate captain.

"Let me go!" she screamed, struggling to pull her arm from the vampire's grasp.

The vampire laughed. Even if he had been a human, he would have been stronger than her. He was bigger, and life at sea made a man strong and hard. But vampires were preternaturally strong. As she struggled, she didn't feel him move an inch. It was as if her arm was encased in concrete.

"Come, girl," he said. "Your new home awaits." He looked deep into her eyes. She felt a warmth wash over her, but she still held back.

The vampire looked at her, confused. "I said, come," he repeated.

Again, she refused to move.

The vampire looked at another human still hiding in the room. "You, come here," he said.

The woman hesitated, but then she did as she was told.

The vampire nodded to himself, seemingly satisfied. "Return to your seat," he said.

Catheryn realized that the vampire had been testing his power. Some very old, very strong vampires possessed a form of hypnotism. It was said to work on humans and witches. He must have been trying to hypnotize her to get her to go with him more easily. But it didn't work. It worked on the other slave, but not Catheryn. She had no idea why, but the vampire didn't seem too concerned by it because he shrugged and resumed trying to get Catheryn to go with him.

As he pulled her toward the door, Catheryn reached out with her free arm for something, anything she could use to free herself. As he dragged her past a small end table, she grabbed a candelabra and struck him over the back of the head with it.

The vampire froze. Everyone in the room seemed to hold their collective breath, waiting to see what he would do. Even Catheryn.

The vampire turned back to her slowly. His eyes were nearly black whereas before they had been a blue the color of the calm sea. While before he had a nearly human shade of skin, he was now sickly pale. Catheryn could verily see the black veins beneath his skin.

He took a menacing step toward her, and she stepped back. He stepped toward her again, and again she retreated, not taking her eyes off him for a moment. Not even blinking. *Blink and you're dead*, she thought.

"Please," she said softly, though she had no idea who she was pleading with.

The vampire took another step, and the floorboard under his foot gave way. He stumbled as he crashed through.

"What the devil?" he asked as he caught himself and pulled his foot back up. He looked at the Hoodoo Queen. "Termites?"

"It is an old house," she replied.

Oddly, the small incident seemed to have distracted the vampire from his hunt. He looked...human again.

"Indeed," the vampire said to the queen. At that, he grabbed Catheryn, tossed her over his shoulder, and quickly walked out of the house.

Catheryn kicked and screamed, but it did no good. In mere moments, she was on the pirate's ship.

She saw other pirates bringing their human captives on board as well. Most of the men and women were trying to fight back, but there was no hope. The pirates simply overpowered and outnumbered them. Some of the humans seemed to have passed out or fallen into some sort of catatonic state. The vampires might have already drunk from them, and they had no energy, or they were in shock. As they were herded below deck like animals, the vampires stared after them hungrily, but they had work to do.

"Raise anchor and hoist the sails," the captain shouted. "I want to be far away from this place as soon as possible, just in case the queen changes her mind."

"Aye-aye, captain," the pirates responded.

The captain hauled Catheryn toward a door under the quarterdeck. He opened it and unceremoniously tossed her inside.

"I'll be back soon," he said. "Don't even think about trying to escape."

She scrambled to her feet and ran toward the door as he slammed it. It locked automatically. She turned the knob and rattled the door, but it wouldn't budge.

The very back of the room was lined with windows. She went to them and tried to open each one. None of them would open even an inch, as though they were glued shut.

She sat down on the bed and debated what to do. This was a

fate worse than death. She would suffer, oh how she would suffer, as the nightly meal of a vampire. Her death would be slow and agonizing.

She held her hands to her throat as she imagined him plunging his fangs into her soft skin, then looked around the room and noticed a pile of straw in the corner and shackles. Was that where he kept his slave? Such cruelty! Even humans when they feasted on the flesh of animals did not prolong their suffering. They would kill the sheep or even a chicken as quickly and painlessly as possible. But she would linger for who knows how long before she finally succumbed to the sweet touch of death.

She stood and looked out the windows again as the ship started to rock. They were headed out to sea. If she didn't escape now, she probably never would.

She held her arms up. "Help me," she said evenly.

Nothing happened.

"Open," she said firmly with more conviction.

But still nothing happened. She dropped her hands and sighed. She didn't know why she was bothering. Her powers probably weren't her own anyway. She must have been imagining it when things happened before. Or they were just coincidences. Witchcraft was innate. A person was born either a witch or a human, and it was simple enough to tell the two apart.

It was not surprising that she, a lowly slave, wished she were more. Wished she had some power. Some control over her life.

The only time she had ever made a decision about her own fate was the last time she saw her sister, Eva. She had sold herself into slavery to protect her, and she had been subject to the whims of the Hoodoo Queen ever since.

Now she was a slave to a vampire.

This couldn't be the end. Such a pathetic end to such a short life. She felt the ship moving faster, bobbing up and down on the water as it pulled farther from shore and deeper out to sea. She raised her hands one last time and called out, "Open, windows! I command you!"

The door to the room opened with a bang, and she turned and saw the pirate captain standing there.

"What are you doing?" he asked.

Her face went hot with embarrassment. She must have looked quite the fool.

The pirate stepped into the room and removed his hat. "We are finally back at sea," he said. "We should be far from NOLA and that hoodoo bitch soon enough." He removed his heavy jacket and stretched his arms. "The men will be calm for now. They will have food and drink…"

Why was he telling her this? she wondered to herself as he continued mumbling. Did he think she was his friend? His lover? Someone who would care what he was thinking, what his stresses of the day were?

She stood stock-still, hoping that he would forget the real reason she was there.

He removed his boots and sat on the bed, rubbing the back of his neck. He motioned for her to come to him.

She shook her head.

"You will make me force you?" he asked tiredly.

"I'll not willingly go to my death," she said.

"What is your name?" he asked.

"Catheryn Beauregard," she said, surprising herself. Why should she give him her name?

"I am Captain Rainier," he said. "And you are now a guest on *The Cursed Storm.*"

Catheryn snorted automatically at the word "guest."

Rainier smiled. "Perhaps that was the wrong word," he said. "But nonetheless, I am captain, and you are my slave. And after I drink from you, you will be my devotee. Do you understand?"

Catheryn nodded. Vampire slaves were often called "devotees" because some people gave themselves willingly to vampires, usually in exchange for protection. But Catheryn balked at this title. She would never willingly devote herself to a vampire. The man who had kidnapped her. The man who would eat her.

"Then come here," he commanded for the second time. "I am... famished." At that, his eyes once again darkened and his skin went pale.

Catheryn shrunk back and shook her head.

The captain sighed. "Why do my commands not work on you?"

Catheryn didn't reply. She didn't have an answer for him.

Finally, he stood and advanced toward her quickly, so quickly she was in his arms with her head pulled back before she could blink.

Then she felt the sharp burst of pain in her neck as he bit. She cried out and tried to throttle him with her fists, but soon she stopped moving.

A feeling of warmth and contentment washed over her. She thought for a moment she might be in a very safe place. But part of her knew where she was and what was happening. The vampire was sucking her blood, and though it might feel pleasurable due to the drug-like venom injected by his fangs for just this purpose, she knew that she could die if he did not stop himself.

"Help me..." she whispered.

But no help came. She closed her eyes, and her body went limp.

CHAPTER 4

The warmth of her blood filled Rainier's mouth. He nearly groaned in pleasure, she was so delicious. But then, he started to see sparks, like fireworks in his eyes. He took a step back and fell to his knees. He looked up, and standing before him was Catheryn. But she did not look like the weak slave he had just been feeding on. She was standing tall and proud, a woman with power.

He shook his head and blinked his eyes, but she still stood there, the wind blowing her long hair. She raised her arm and pointed at...something. He couldn't tell what. Her mouth opened, and something like a battle cry passed through her lips. Then the shouts of countless other voices all rang out: "Catheryn! Catheryn!"

"Catheryn!" he gasped as he opened his eyes. He was standing just where he was before, in front of the window, holding Catheryn's limp body in his arms.

"What have I done?" he asked, his hands trembling.

He had no idea how long he had been drinking. He didn't want to kill her—at least not yet. She had to sustain him for who knew how long until they found a new supply of humans. But that vision, those sparks. He didn't realize what he was doing, what was happening.

She moaned, and Rainier breathed a sigh. She was still alive. He stepped back, still holding her, feeling just as weak—no, even more weak—than before. Why had she not rejuvenated him? What was wrong with her?

He picked her drooping body up in his arms and moved her to the pile of straw on the floor, then laid her down and tossed a blanket over her. Afterward, he lied on his own bed and promptly passed out.

∽

When Rainier woke hours later, his full strength still had not returned. He rubbed his head and sat up slowly. Swayed a bit. He almost felt...hungover. A sensation he had not experienced since he was human. He looked over in the corner and saw Catheryn sitting on her straw, her blanket pulled tight around her.

"What are you?" he asked.

Her eyes widened. "What do you mean?"

"Your blood," he said. "There is...something wrong with it. Why am I not rejuvenated?"

She shrugged. "I don't know. I am just a worthless slave. Would the Hoodoo Queen have let you take me so easily if I was anything special?"

She had a point. Of course there were all manner of strange things in the world. Vampires and witches were known to exist; could there be other supernatural beings that even a century after the Rift still had not been discovered? Or what if...

What if were humans *evolving*?

Many species adapted to change over time, and the world had certainly changed.

He would have to keep his eye on her, see if she exhibited any other strange signs or behaviors. He was glad he had been the one to select her, as opposed to another crewmember. He was strong. Even in a weakened state, he was stronger than anyone else. But his crew, he needed them to be in top fighting form.

After standing and removing his clothes, he used a basin of warm water to wash himself. It did not bother him to be in a state of undress in front of his slave. What was she to him? It was nothing more than a cat or dog being in the room. Someone he would give attention to her when he wished. He did steal a glance at her in a mirror, though, and he thought he caught her staring at him. He stood a little taller at that.

After he dressed and donned his hat, his sword belt, and his holster for his flintlock pistols, he turned to Catheryn.

"Do not attempt to escape," he ordered. "Do you understand?"

She nodded, but did not speak.

"If you do, I will clap you in those irons."

She still did not reply, but turned to stare at the wall. He was about to leave when he heard a low rumbling sound. Catheryn rubbed her stomach.

"Are you hungry?" he asked.

She shook her head.

"Come now, girl. Don't be foolish. I can't have you starving to death. I need you to retain your strength. Both of our lives depend on it."

She looked up at him, and he tried to give her a reassuring smile.

"You mean to prolong my suffering?" she asked.

"Certainly not," he said. "The bite was not wholly unpleasant, was it? Some humans say it is actually pleasurable. The vampire's embrace, they call it. As long as I feed responsibly and you take care of your health, you can still live a long life."

"As a food source," she said. "What kind of life is that? One where I sit on this pile of straw and service you when you call?"

"This isn't new to you. You were a slave long before you came to me, were you not?" he asked. "Does it really matter if you serve the Hoodoo Queen or me? This is your fate. You should accept that and learn to find your place in this new world you have found yourself in."

He nearly found himself reciting the serenity prayer: God, give me the serenity to accept the things I cannot change, the courage to change the things I can, and the wisdom to know the difference.

He'd been raised Catholic, and his grandmother had shared that prayer with him many times. He'd recited it enough times to have it ingrained in his mind yet still, despite him having learned as an adult that prayer was not actually in the bible.

That was lifetimes ago now. He'd left his religion behind over a century ago...along with his humanity.

The woman opened her mouth as if to speak again, but then closed her mouth and turned away again. Her stomach grumbled once more.

Rainier couldn't help but smile. She was strong, but she was only human. She would have to learn to depend on him to survive. Eventually, they would form a symbiotic relationship, each of them relying on the other. Of course, she didn't realize the power she held over him. After all, she held his life in her hands, too. But he wouldn't tell her that. He had to maintain the illusion of control.

Besides, the girl wasn't a completely unpleasant companion. She was feisty and easy on the eyes. He would make sure she was well taken care of.

"I'll have some food brought for you anyway," he said. "Take care of yourself. You have free reign of my quarters, but don't venture out. I wouldn't trust the other men."

He left and locked the door behind him.

It was a foggy morning. The sun could barely be seen through the thick of it. The barrelman in the crow's nest couldn't see more with a spyglass than his own eyes. But the men on deck certainly seemed more refreshed and in higher spirits. He approached just as a small group were tossing one of the humans overboard. His body was so desiccated he hardly looked human at all.

"What happened?" Rainier asked.

Mathis approached. "Sorry, captain," he said. "One of the men lost control. Sucked the poor bastard dry."

"See to it the man is punished," Rainier ordered. "We need this supply to last a while."

"He's already been locked down below, sir," the mate replied.

"Bring him to the deck and have him whipped. Make a public example of him."

"Aye-aye, sir," Mathis said and headed off to carry out the order.

The rest of the ship seemed much calmer and in order. The men went about their business, securing riggings, swabbing the deck, and keeping an eye out through the fog for anything of note.

Indeed, a well-fed crew was a well-behaved crew.

He headed up to check on the helmsman.

"How goes it?" Rainier asked.

The helmsman grunted. "An ill morning, sir," he said. "Can't see nothing. Traveling at a snail's pace. I keep saying we should only allow male bloodbags on board. It's always bad luck to have a woman aboard, even ones that just serve as food."

He patted the old vampire on the shoulder with a chuckle. If the old man ever found out that several of the ship's crewmen were actually crewwomen in disguise, he'd probably have an ulcer. There were even some vampire pirate ships that were crewed *only* by women, and they seemed to have no more problems than any other pirate crew. While human women had a reputation for being weaker than men, vampire and witch women were on a much more even keel with their male counterparts, having access to the same supernatural elements.

Rainier stepped up to the railing and breathed in the morning sea air. He let the saltiness fill his lungs and the wind lightly caress his face. There was no other feeling like it in the world. He'd been a seaman for as long as he could remember, even when he was human.

There were no human pirates anymore, though. They simply couldn't survive against the vampires once they took to the seas.

A pirate's life for me, Rainier thought to himself.

A whistling sound brought him out of his reverie. At first, he thought it was one of men on deck whistling while he worked, but he quickly realized that the sound meant danger.

"Hit the deck!" he yelled just as a cannon ball slammed into the water next to the ship, sending a small wave over the edge.

"Stations!" Rainier yelled, and like a well-oiled machine, the men got to work. They immediately set to their assigned tasks, each one knowing exactly what was required of him.

The helmsman steered the ship away from the direction the cannonball had come, but it was too late. The attacking ship suddenly cut its way through the fog and pulled up alongside. The ship's men were ready to attack. They were already dressed and armed, their muskets loaded. They were holding up planks, ready to drop them so they could cross over, and men up above in the rigging gripped ropes, preparing to swing across from one ship to the other.

"Arm yourselves! Ready the cannons!" Rainier shouted.

To their credit, his men did not dawdle. They knew what was expected of them and what was necessary if they wanted to survive this fight.

"Rainier!"

Rainier's blood stopped cold in his veins as the familiar female voice rent the air. Maybe the helmsman wasn't so wrong about women being bad luck. Rainier slowly raised his head just above the railing so he could see the owner of the voice.

The other ship's captain leaned over the railing of her ship, her cutlass raised high. Her auburn hair whipped around her like a wild banshee, and even from this distance, he could see the wildness in her blazing green eyes.

"Rainier!" she shouted again as caught him in her sights. "Prepare to be boarded."

CHAPTER 5

After the pirate left Catheryn alone, she felt like she could breathe for the first time since the pirates entered the Hoodoo House. She rubbed her neck where the vampire had bitten her. It felt as though the wound had already healed. Surprisingly, she felt fine physically. She thought she would feel groggy and exhausted after a feeding, but she felt alert instead. She was hungry, though, even if she wouldn't admit it to...what did he call himself? Rainier.

What an obnoxious, self-righteous boor! He acted as though he was doing her some sort of kindness by allowing her to sleep on his floor and then ordering her food.

Maybe he was.

It could certainly be worse. She could be one of her poor fellow slaves who were locked up below and had to feed the whole crew.

A knock rattled the door, and a small hole in the wood opened as a tray was pushed through. She walked over and took the meal. The food, simple as it was, smelled divine. It was just a bowl of grits drizzled with honey and a cup of juice, but since she hadn't eaten since the day before, it tasted like food fit for a queen. She slowly savored each bite and then licked the bowl clean.

After she ate, she explored the room a bit to see what she could find out about her present situation. She walked over to a desk and rifled through the papers a bit. There were several maps. They looked to be of varying ages, as if tracking the changes in the world over time.

Many years ago, the world was fairly unified. There were only seven continents, and all of them could be accessed by sea. But after the Rift, the great calamity caused by the unholy union between a vampire and a witch, the world had fractured. There were now sixteen divisions, each one protected by a magical shield provided by the most powerful witches in that division. The shields also kept anyone from traveling from one division to another.

Although the divisions were able to communicate somewhat via old CB radios, they didn't always work. She examined the maps a bit more, and it looked as if Rainier's crew had been exploring the very edges of the NOLA shield. Were they looking for a way through? She laughed to herself. *That* would never happen. For such vicious pirates, they were certainly foolish buffoons.

She moved one of the papers aside and found a small leather-bound book. Upon opening it, she realized it was a diary. *Rainier's* diary! He had not written in it since he brought her on board, but he had the day before.

Today we ran out of food. We have no choice but to return to NOLA and raid for humans.

Our latest trip to the Edge was just as fruitless as all the others. Many of the men fear we will never find a way through the Shield, never connect to the other divisions. While our division is surviving for now, it is only doing that, no more. It is not thriving. The food output for the humans and witches is slowly declining. The waters are rising. The human numbers are dwindling. It might take decades, but eventually, our division will no longer be inhabitable. We must find a way through. Must find a way to connect to the rest of the world.

I fear the crew is losing its faith and hope in not just the mission, but me as well. Even though there is no one who could lead them better, any failures fall on my shoulders.

How much longer will they allow me to lead them, when even I am unsure where I am going?

Heavy wears the crown, Catheryn thought. Even bloodthirsty monsters had to contend with the stresses of daily life. But was it true what he had written? Was NOLA slowly dying? As a slave, she wasn't kept abreast of the larger concerns of the area. She lived only day to day, purely in survival mode. But the Hoodoo Queen had recently decreased the slaves' daily rations. She had been so hungry...all of them were...

The day before

Catheryn rummaged around the pantry. The cook was at market, and the other servants were all out running errands, but they would be back soon. The Hoodoo House was home to many, many people. You were never alone for long.

The queen had cut the slaves' daily food allotment by nearly a third. It wasn't enough. They were all so hungry. Some more than others. Many of the adults were sharing their rations with the children, but they couldn't survive on such meager food stores for long.

Catheryn held a burlap sack as she picked through the kitchen's fresh supplies—the fruits, the vegetables, the loaves of bread. She only took one or two of each thing, hoping they wouldn't go missing that way. She was leerier of taking any canned goods. The cook probably kept a better inventory of those kinds of items.

Two potatoes, one carrot, several handfuls of rice, a few rolls, a small bag of flour. Was there any way she could smuggle out just a small amount of oil?

As she rifled through one cabinet, looking for a small jar she could use, a voice spoke abruptly behind her.

"What do you think you are doing?" a woman asked.

Catheryn turned and saw a young witch.

"I asked you a question, slave," the woman said.

"I'm just..." Catheryn floundered. "Cook told me to help prepare the daily rations for the slaves..."

The woman stepped over and grabbed the bag, opening it. "Are you stealing?" she asked.

Catheryn could not reply.

The woman's face contorted. "I'll just have to ask cook about this!"

Catheryn couldn't let that happen. There had to be some way to stop her.

At that, a knife that had been sitting on the counter flew across the room and stabbed the woman in the arm, and she screamed.

"Oh my God! Oh my God! What..." She cast her eyes around the room, as though looking for her invisible assailant.

Catheryn looked, too. Was there someone else in the room? Had she done that? She couldn't let the woman expose her. She's be whipped to death for stealing!

Finally, the young witch pulled the knife from her arm and dropped it. She held her hand over her wound to staunch the bleeding, and her eyes landed back on Catheryn. "You!" she nearly screeched. "What are you? You're nothing but a slave! How did you...what did you...I'm going right to the queen. She's take care of this right now!"

The woman turned quick on her heels and headed for the door.

Catheryn's fight instincts kicked in, and she ran after the witch. She grabbed her by the shoulder and spun her around. The witch shot at Catheryn with a burst of energy, which sent her flying backward, and she landed on her backside. The witch turned again toward the door, but Catheryn raised her hand.

"Stop!" she said. A cast iron skillet that had been hanging from a hook above her suddenly fell free and hit the woman in the head. She crumpled to the floor.

Catheryn held her hand to her mouth. She couldn't believe what had just happened. Was she dead? Had she killed a witch?

She slowly inched over to the woman's body and checked her pulse. *Still alive.* Catheryn wasn't sure if that was better or worse. She dragged the witch over to the pantry and secured it closed with a broom, then grabbed a cloth and wiped the blood from the floor. But it didn't matter. She would be caught. The witch would expose her. She'd be revealed as a thief and an attempted murderess. The Hoodoo Queen would have no choice but to put her to death.

Catheryn couldn't see a way out of this mess. She forgot about her bag of food and ran to her nook under the stairs and tried to come up with a plan.

And then, the pirates attacked.

Out of the frying pan and into the fire, Catheryn mused. She sighed as she walked to the widows and looked out. How was she going to get out of this mess? And if she did, what then?

One step at a time, girl.

First, she needed to get off this ship. It didn't matter if she escaped at another port or ended up on a desert island, she just needed to get away.

Boom!

The explosion sounded very close. The ship rocked hard to one side, then the other. She struggled to maintain her balance. Got on her hands and knees and crawled to the door. Peeking out, she saw another ship had pulled up alongside *The Cursed Storm*, and several pirates swung on ropes from the other ship to this one. More explosions boomed from cannons being fired. Considering the way the ship rumbled, she knew some of the shots were being fired from this ship...and other *at* this ship.

Then, she saw him.

Captain Rainier ran up to one of the pirates that had landed on the ship, sliced through him easily, and tipped him over the side of ship. He turned and slashed another pirate that had hoped to stab him in the back. One after another, Rainier cut down his enemy. Catheryn couldn't help but be impressed with his skill.

Then, a woman dressed similar to Rainier approached him. She carried herself with equal surety, and the two exchanged words before they assumed their fighting stances. It appeared Rainier had finally met his match. She must have been the captain from the other ship.

Catheryn was enjoying watching the two of them dance. So much so that she almost forgot she should be afraid. What if Rainier was defeated? This new band of pirates would take Catheryn and the others away. The devil you know is better than the devil you don't, after all. A small voice in her throat cheered Rainier on.

She didn't even notice that two other pirates who were fighting were getting closer and closer to the door. Not until they smashed through it.

Catheryn gasped as she jumped to the side. Scrambling to hide, she ducked behind the desk as the two pirates fought. It was clear the pirate from Rainier's ship was losing, and before Catheryn could even consider intervening, the attacking pirate ran the other one through.

Catheryn stayed quiet, hoping the pirate would run off and join the battle elsewhere, but she had no such luck.

"Ah, just what we're looking for," the pirate said with a greasy smile.

Of course, Catheryn thought.

She jumped to her feet and quickly ran past the pirate and out the door. He must have been expecting her to cower instead of flee, because he stood stunned for a moment before reacting.

"Come back here, you!" she heard him yell from behind her.

But Catheryn was already running across the main deck toward the grate that led below deck. Once again, she found herself trying to free her fellow slaves. If they could sneak away while the pirates were busy fighting each other, maybe they could steal a lifeboat and row away before anyone noticed. Or at least before any of them could do anything about it.

The grating was open, so she slipped inside quickly and slid down the ladder. There were now pirates fighting below deck as well. Some of the pirates were chasing and catching the human slaves, trying to drag them above deck. They must have heard about Rainier's raid on the Hoodoo House and wanted the slaves for themselves. For a moment, Catheryn wondered if all the vampire pirates, or even all the vampires in NOLA, were running out of humans to feed on.

If that was the case, Catheryn and her fellow humans wouldn't be safe anywhere. They would always be hunted.

But she couldn't worry about that right now. She had to focus on trying to escape. She lifted a sword off a fallen pirate and turned to one who was trying to drag a female slave toward the ladder up to the main deck. Catheryn used all her strength to run the pirate through from behind. He slumped over and then crumbled to the ground.

"Catheryn!" the woman gasped. "Where have you been?"

"No time!" Catheryn yelled. "We have to escape. Get up to the main deck and try to find a lifeboat we can escape in!"

The woman nodded and ran up the ladder. Catheryn tried to pull her sword out of the dead pirate, but it was stuck.

"Hey you!" she heard. She turned to face the pirate from earlier in Rainier's quarters. "Got ya!"

Catheryn backed up, unarmed...and cornered.

CHAPTER 6

Pirates from the other ship swung over to *The Dark Storm*, including the opposing pirate captain. As the ships got closer to each other, gangplanks were lowered and the enemy pirates swarmed the ship like locusts.

"It's been too long, Captain Rainier," the woman with red hair said as she approached.

"Not long enough, Rene," he said as the two circled one another.

"That's Captain Lacroix to you," she said as she tapped his sword with her own. "That's always been the trouble with you. No respect."

Rainier watched his men from over her shoulder and was pleased to see they were holding their own. Rainier trained them hard for just such an occasion.

"What's brings you here, Captain Lacroix?" he asked. "You know your scrappers are no match for my hard trained men."

"No respect but plenty of confidence," Rene replied. "That's what I always did like about you." She advanced and thrusted her sword toward him. Rainier easily deflected her blow and moved to the side. He then advanced and parried, forcing her to retreat a few steps.

"Call off your men, Rene," he said. "This is pointless."

"Give me what I want, Rainier," she demanded and struck again.

"And what is that?" he asked as he deflected.

"Your humans," she said. "You know how rare it is to find humans on the high seas or even near the coasts anymore. They've all fled inland. We need the humans you stole from the Hoodoo Queen."

"Not on your life," he said. "I have my own crew to look after."

"And I have mine," she said. "I can either kill you and take your humans, or you can hand over your humans willingly and look for more elsewhere. You might survive if you hand them over."

Rainier doubted that. Rene Lacroix was as bloodthirsty as they come, in more than one sense. She was a vampire as well, but she was also a violent and merciless pirate. She was not above slaughtering other pirate crews simply to lessen the competition. She had no sense of professional curtesy.

"We made a rather fierce team at one point," Rainier said. "Remember all that time we spent together, ridding the seas of the human pirates that once tried to sail as though they had a chance? Now look at you. Picking a fight with someone you can't beat all for a few scraps of blood."

After the human pirates had all been killed or ran aground, the vampire pirates started turning on each other. That's when Rainier and Rene had to part ways. He couldn't trust her to not stab him in the back if it would benefit her in some way.

"Look at you, trying to prey on my feminine sensibilities," Rene mocked. "Must mean you don't have as much faith in the strength of your crew as you once did." She advanced and struck at him, hard. She practically stomped with each advance and grunted with each thrust of her sword.

Rainier had to be cautious as he fought her off. She had an anger, a desperation to her fight. He wasn't sure why. As far as he knew, he hadn't wronged her in any meaningful way, at least not lately, and he hadn't heard of her having any skirmishes with any other pirate crews.

How long it had been since she and her crew had human blood to drink? If she and her men were desperate for food, that could explain her furor.

"I don't want to have to hurt you, Rene," Rainier said as he continued to let her advance. He was only on the defense right now, looking for an opening, testing her for weakness.

"Hurt *me?*" she asked. "I'm winning!" she screamed as she brought her sword down on his.

Out of the corner of his eye, Rainier saw a flash of black curls. He turned to see Catheryn running across the deck toward the hatch that led down below. She must have been trying to reach the other slaves.

"Bloody hell," he muttered.

Rene turned as well. Her pupils grow big, like a cat who had caught sight of a mouse. Her mouth gaped, and Rainier could have sworn he saw her start to drool.

Rene took off toward Catheryn, and Rainier followed Rene. Rene was much faster than Catheryn, but Rainier was quicker than both of them. As Catheryn reached the hatch and started down the ladder, Rene reached for her. But she was wide open. Rainier easily slammed into her, knocking her onto her back.

The vampires moved so quickly, and Catheryn was so determined to reach the other slaves, Rainier thought Catheryn never even saw the danger she was in as she quickly disappeared below deck.

"I'll kill you!" Rene bellowed as she attempted to scramble to her feet.

Rainier decided that Rene was indeed out of her mind with

hunger. If there wasn't such a shortage of humans, he would have almost felt pity for her. He was certainly not above helping a fellow pirate in need if he thought it might benefit him in some way later. But he didn't see any way that helping Rene now wouldn't put him and his men at risk. They were down to eight humans to share for the whole crew, and they wouldn't last long. And Rene was right. The humans were fleeing the shores and heading inland, both to escape pirate raids and the rising waters. Even he wasn't exactly sure where he was going to find the next supply of humans for his own crew.

Rainier grabbed Rene around the collar and threw her into the railing of his ship. He used all his strength to pin her down. She reached into her belt and pulled out a dagger, but Rainier grabbed her wrist. He pounded her arm on the railing to make her let go, but she kneed him in the crotch, causing him to flinch. She cuffed him on the side of the head with the hilt of the knife, and Rainier stumbled back.

"Yield," Rene said as she pointed her sword and knife at Rainier. "Yield and you may live, though I can't make any promises."

"It's you who'll be begging for mercy in a moment," Rainier said.

"Defiant to the end," she said as she took a step forward. "I like that. I always did like—Ahh!"

Rene screamed as a bullet penetrated her shoulder. She screamed, dropped her sword, and clutched at the wound. She and Rainier both turned toward where the shot had come from. Rainier's first mate, Mathis, stood with the rifle still pointed at Rene. Rainier scanned the deck. While the fighting between the two crews was still intense, it was clear that Rainier's men had the upper hand.

Rene looked back at Rainier just as Rainier plowed into her, shoving her hard against the railing and knocking the breath out of her. He then reached down, grabbed her leg and flipped her over the side of the ship. Rainier couldn't help but watch with glee as Rene fell several stories, screaming all the way, and splashed into the water below. She came back up to the surface of the water with gasps and one flailing arm.

"The sea water will help clear that wound right up for you!" he shouted down to her.

She responded by flipping him off.

Rainier couldn't help but laugh, but Mathis called him back to attention.

"Sir!" he yelled. "Your orders?"

"Take care of these scallywags!" he said. He headed below deck to find out what had become of Catheryn.

The fighting below deck was fierce as well, but there were not as many fighters as above deck. Rainier made his way through the lower decks with ease, lending his sword to his crew who had already made good work of the invaders.

Finally, his gaze fell on Catheryn, who cowered in a far off dark corner, blocked by a rival pirate. Rainier bolted toward them with his full speed, planning to run the fellow through, but just as he was about to strike, a heavy beam fell, crushing the pirate.

"What the devil?" he asked as he looked from the dead man up to where the beam had fallen and finally to Catheryn.

"Termites?" she asked.

"Not bloody likely," Rainier said. "Termites on a pirate ship? Can you imagine? A single hole could sink the whole ship!"

She shrugged. "Must have been loose, then."

"It's a load bearing beam!" he said.

She shrugged again, as though she had no idea what he was talking about.

"It...It's an important beam that is connected to the structure of the whole ship. The mizzen mast is up above it. We won't be able to sail until it's fixed. We wouldn't have *been* sailing if it had been in need of repair."

"It must have come loose in the cannon fire," she suggested.

Rainier stared at her. She was so calm, so collected, considering she had just faced a deadly pirate and nearly been crushed by a beam. They were still under attack as well; the fighting up above still echoed in clangs of metal and cries of falling men above them. Why was she not more concerned?

"Did…did you have anything to do with this?" he asked, pointing his sword to the beam.

"What do you mean?" she asked.

"Are you…are you a witch? Tell me now."

"No," she said. "I'm not a witch. The Hoodoo Queen…"

"Yeah, yeah, the Hoodoo Queen wouldn't have let you go. But there is…something isn't right about you."

She shrugged again. "People have been telling me that my whole life."

Rainier grabbed her by the wrist and led her over to the ladder that went back to the upper levels. He surveyed the damage as they went. He had lost a few men, but not many, and the cannons had certainly done some damage. They would need to find a port soon in order to make repairs.

He ordered his men to round up the humans and let him know if any of them had been kidnapped or killed or if any escaped. Then Rainier took Catheryn back to the main deck.

By now, the fighting had stopped, and Lacroix's men had retreated to her ship. He stood at the railing and watched as she pulled away. Rene was watching him as well.

We will meet again, she mouthed.

He was sure they would.

"Captain," Mathis said as he approached. "Two of the humans were killed in the attack, and it looks like Lacroix's men were able to steal two more."

"And then there were four," he said, shaking his head.

His men would not survive on so few humans for more than a few days. And the poor humans would be sucked dry. There would be no way to preserve them the way he hoped to preserve Catheryn.

Catheryn.

Once the men ran out of their own rations, they would certainly be looking to her. Even though she wouldn't sustain the lot of them for more than a day, the men would not see reason. Hunger makes monsters of even the most rational of men. To keep her to himself would be seen as selfish, so unlike a leader.

"What are your orders, sir?"

"We can't head to any of the pirate havens," Rainier said. "By now, all of them will know about our humans. We will be targets for any crew suffering from a blood shortage."

"We can head for the shoals near Revenge Bay," the mate said. "It's shallow and has lots of trees nearby for timber."

Rainier nodded. "Make for Revenge Bay."

"Aye-aye, sir!" Mathis said.

Rainier grabbed Catheryn's hand and headed back to his quarters. He was quite distraught when he saw the state it was in.

"What the hell happened?" he asked.

"Two pirates were fighting and knocked down the door," Catheryn explained. "Then one of them came after me, so I took off."

"Were you injured?" he asked, looking her up and down.

"No," she said, looking at him as if confused.

Rainier backed off. "Oh, well, good, then." He wasn't exactly sure why he was acting so concerned either. But part of him wanted to rip that pirate who had cornered her into bits himself. "I wouldn't want my supply damaged," he added quickly, though he knew that wasn't the real reason for the concern he couldn't place his finger on.

He sighed to himself, realizing one of the emotions he was feeling right now was one he hadn't felt in a long time. Perhaps since he was a human.

Jealously.

He was jealous that the stupid beam had robbed him of the chance to protect her, to keep her safe. She was his property. It was his job to make sure no one hurt her.

"As long as you are in my possession," Rainier said, "I won't let any harm come to you."

"Except for the harm you inflict yourself?" she asked. "You know, when you eat me?"

"As I've said before, the vampire's embrace doesn't have to be painful or deadly. You should let me show you."

Catheryn recoiled, taking a few steps back. But she was stopped by his large bed.

"I...I'm exhausted from two solid days of fighting and hardly having anything to eat," he said. "I need to feed."

He took a few slow steps toward her until he was right in front of her. Her eyes were wide with terror...and something else. He could sense her heart beating rapidly and hear her shallow breaths. She was afraid, yes, but also excited.

He reached up and ran his finger along her cheek. She gasped. She turned her head away, but left her neck completely exposed to him. He could see the warm blood pulsing in her neck. He ran his finger along her neck and thought he heard her release a barely audible moan.

"Do you want me to bite you, Catheryn?" he asked.

She hesitated, but then she nodded.

Rainier lowered his head to her neck, where he gave her a couple of sweet kisses, then a lick, tasting her saltiness. When her breath hitched and a trembled shuddered through her small frame, he finally bit.

She gasped, loudly this time, but not out of pain. Her warm blood gushed into his mouth, and he sucked eagerly, wrapping his arms around her and holding her close to him as he drank from her deeply.

But then, he saw sparks.

As he raised his head, he saw not Catheryn, but the Hoodoo

Queen. She and her coven of witches were scouring NOLA for humans, rounding them up and putting them into cages.

Rainier closed his eyes, shaking himself out of the vision. He released Catheryn from the embrace, but she was already asleep. He laid her on the bed and then collapsed beside her.

CHAPTER 7

Catheryn lay in the bed, staring at the ceiling. She wasn't tired, but she didn't feel a pressing need to get out of bed just yet.

When she woke, she was surprised she was laying in the bed and not on her hay bale, but she didn't think Rainier had violated her. Well, other than drinking her blood. He must have simply been too tired from the fight to move her from the bed to the hay.

He was gone now, and he hadn't left her any orders, not even to clean his room. Is this what it would be like if she accepted her place with him? The leisurely life of a pirate's lady? She had been a slave for so long, she was used to being up at dawn and working until late at night, sore and exhausted from the day. She couldn't remember the last time she woke up and didn't immediately have to get up and start working.

At least it gave her a few minutes to think. What exactly was happening to her? She expected to feel exhausted after the vampire fed on her, and while she did pass out at first, she now felt...energized. Invigorated. Powerful. As if she could deal with any adversity standing in her path.

Could it be related to Rainier feeding on her? He did mention that after he fed on her he felt weaker when he should feel stronger. While he was sucking her blood, was she sucking his... energy? His life force? His qi?

Whatever it was, she knew her magic was getting stronger as well. She caused that beam to fall. She knew it was no mere accident or coincidence this time. But could she do it again?

She sat up in the bed and looked around the room. It was still in a disaster state, but the door had been repaired at least. Rainier must have ordered it done while she was still sleeping.

She pointed toward a tipped over chair and willed it to right itself. "Move," she said.

Nothing happened.

She stood and tried again. "Move, you stupid chair," she ordered.

The chair sat still.

Catheryn grunted, annoyed. She had definitely caused that beam to fall. And she was certainly feeling stronger. But she seemed to have no control over the power coursing within her.

She didn't feel as if she was lying when she told Rainier she wasn't a witch. If she was a witch, she should know. The Hoodoo Queen should have known. She should be able to harness her powers.

That she had magical powers was certain, but what kind of powers exactly, where they came from, and what it meant for her were all questions she still had no answers to. Maybe she was not witch, nor vampire, nor human.

Maybe she was something else entirely.

Catheryn wasn't going to get any answers hiding out in the captain's quarters all day. She walked over to the door and looked out the window. Everything seemed back to normal. The sun was shining, and the pirates were going about their work. She turned the handle. To her surprise, it wasn't locked. She left the safety of the captain's quarters and walked along the deck.

The pirates paid her little mind as she passed them. They all seemed to have a clear job to do and weren't staring at her like they were dying for a meal. Most of them ignored her, and the few who did look at her just put their knuckle to their forehead as a polite way to mimic doffing their hat had they had one. A few mumbled "ma'am" or "miss" as she passed. It was as though she was simply a guest.

That won't last long, she mused to herself. She might not know much about Rainier's world, but she knew these vampires were hungry and had little food. At some point, might they be hungry enough to turn on Rainier to get to her?

She pushed the thought away. That day was not today, and she hoped to be far away from this ship by time that day came.

She strolled to the railing and stood there, breathing in the salty sea air and soaking in the sun. As she looked out, all she could see was the blue of the ocean. No land, no other ships in sight. The ship gently rocked forward and back. It was so peaceful, she could see why some people were drawn to the sea.

She finally caught sight of Captain Rainier up on the quarterdeck with the helmsman. He caught sight of her as well. Instead of looking angry that she was out of his quarters, he gave a small smile and nod. She climbed the steps up to the helm.

"Morning, captain," she said politely.

"Miss Catheryn," he replied. "You look refreshed."

"I slept like the dead," she said, then put her hand to her mouth. "Oh, that is…I mean…"

Rainier laughed. "No need to apologize. It's common to need a good rest after a feeding."

She blushed, remembering the way he held her in his arms as he fed and the touch of his lips on her neck. Her fingers automatically went to the spot on her neck where he had bitten her, but once again, she felt no wounds.

"Don't worry," he said. "A vampire's bite always heals when we are done. It's a...survival trick of sorts. Back when vampires were still a secret, we couldn't leave track marks everywhere or we would have been discovered."

"Are you that old?" she asked. "Do you remember when the vampires and witches still had to hide themselves?"

He chuckled. "A vampire has to keep some secrets," he said. "It's the only mystery we have left."

She pursed her lips, pondering the answer to her own question. How old was he? How long he had been a vampire? But he was right; she'd be wasting her time to even ask. He wasn't going to just tell her his life story. But certainly she could get some answers from him, such as how the pirates could be on deck in the sunlight.

"The sun," she said. "It doesn't hurt you?"

"It used to," he said. "According to the oldest vampires, the Berkano, before the Rift, they couldn't go out in sunlight at all. But after the world changed, the vampires changed, too. Sunlight can be a bit irritating to some, but not really life-threatening."

"And the crosses?" she asked. "When I held the stakes like a cross, you simply knocked them away. Did that change to?"

He laughed. "I don't think crosses ever bothered vampires. But it's a silly enough myth. Why not let people keep thinking it?"

Catheryn couldn't help but smile at how silly she must have looked trying to ward him off with her sticks. She was lucky to be alive.

"So, where are we heading?" she asked.

"A place called Revenge Bay," he said. "It's shallow with lots of trees, so we can make repairs. But we will probably make a stop on the way. There are rumors that a new human village has popped up along the shore nearby. We can hopefully find more food there."

"Food?" she snapped, her anger returning to her in a flash. "More humans to feed off, you mean."

"Naturally," he said. "Well, regular food as well. Nothing beats a good roasted leg of lamb, does it? You enjoy that oatmeal in your belly, yes? And fresh oranges to keep you from getting sick? Where do you think we get that sort of stuff on the high seas?"

"*Trading* for goods is hardly the same as kidnapping and feeding off human beings," she said. "It's perfectly possible to live a life at sea that doesn't result in stealing and slaughtering innocents."

"How do you know so much about life as a vampire and a pirate?" he asked. "How much time have you spent as either? How much time have you spent trying to live a life like this and be responsible for more hundreds of people who depend on you?"

Catheryn crossed her arms. "Of course I know nothing about the day to day managerial process of running a vampire pirate ship. But this way of life is cruel. And what's worse, it's unsustainable. You said yourself that there are not enough humans to sustain the pirates. The humans are leaving the shores. Their numbers are also dwindling. There has to be better ways of surviving than this. You need the human race to survive. What will you do when they are gone?"

Rainier grunted. "The mighty lion does not concern himself with the worries of the gazelle."

"He might if there suddenly were no gazelle," Catheryn responded. "But you are no lion. You are a thinking, reasoning… person." She had to stop herself from saying human. "You need to consider the future."

"Thank you for your lecture, Miss Catheryn," he said. "But I also have to think about the here and now. And now, my men are hungry. Another human died in the night from injuries she received during the fight. I have over a hundred men and only three humans to feed them. It won't be long before they turn their hungry fangs on you."

"You *stole* me and made me your private food bank. Don't

pretend you are planning this raid as some gift for me, as a protection," she said.

"You might not like it, but that is how it is," the captain responded. "I am a vampire. I must drink blood to survive. Until you come up with a viable alternative to that fact, I think you should keep your opinions on how vampires survive to yourself."

Catheryn huffed. She turned on her heels and headed back to his quarters.

She was mad, even if she knew he was right. In fact, they were both right. Vampires needed to feed on humans to survive, but they needed to find a better way for the humans to survive.

She had a feeling Rainier was not an unthinking beast. He knew she was right. But even if she managed to change his mind, there were countless vampires in the world. She couldn't change the mind of every vampire in the division, or on the planet, anytime soon.

In the meantime, she'd do well to remember what brought her here. Rainier was not a lover. He was her enemy and her captor.

~

That night, all the lights on the ship were extinguished as it approached the human village. The pirates lowered the lifeboats into the water and silently rowed toward shore.

Catheryn watched from the deck of the ship. Rainier ordered her to stay put. She thought about screaming or even setting the ship on fire. Anything to alert the village that the pirates were coming. But there were still some vampires on the ship; not many, but a few. Rainier said if she gave them any trouble to cage her below with the others. So for now, she stayed quiet.

It was so dark that the pirates eventually blended into the pitch black, leaving her unable to see them as they approached the shore. But after several minutes, she heard it: the first screams from the village.

In only a moment, the whole village was alert. People and vampires ran along the shore and through the houses.

The few vampires who were still stuck on the ship watched, grinning nearly ear to ear. They seemed to have forgotten their work as they laughed and pointed at the poor victims as they were captured, killed, or eaten as they tried to escape or fight back.

Catheryn was horrified. No matter how charming Rainier could be, he was just another vampire. Another monster. She had to escape. She couldn't stay here. Rainier and his men had taken all the lifeboats with them to the village and had hidden them in a cove near the village. But the ship wasn't far from the shore.

"Where you think you're goin'?" one of her minders asked as she slipped away.

"Just back to my room," she said. "I can't watch this."

The vampires laughed at that, but they didn't stop her.

She went to her room and grabbed a small bag. She filled with the few foodstuffs she could find—some bread, cheese, oranges—and also grabbed one of the large pieces of splintered wood that was still cluttered around the room. Then she slipped back out of the room and went to the side of the deck away from where the pirates were watching the raid.

She clamored over the side and dropped the wood into the water below before climbing down the rope ladder and placing her pack on the board. Holding onto the board, she lowered herself into the water, then kicked herself toward the shore.

She had to stay out of the line of sight of the pirates on the ship, so she ended up in the woods a bit of a distance from the village. She would have to pass through the village to end up in the cove on the other side where the pirates had docked their lifeboats before attacking the village. She would simply sneak around the village, get to the cove, steal a lifeboat, and row herself to freedom. It was a perfect plan, right?

Heading in the direction she thought would lead her around the village, she soon realized the village was much larger than she expected. It was practically a town. There were cobblestone streets and large buildings—nothing like the thatched houses near the shore. How did such a place exist, and thrive, for so long without the vampires or witches finding them?

For now, she couldn't puzzle that out. She needed to find her way through and escape.

As she slipped from shadow to shadow, she estimated she was about halfway through the town when she heard, "There's one!"

She looked up and saw that two of the pirates had spotted her and were headed straight for her. *Shit!* In a rush, she ran into the nearest building, entering so quickly that she forgot to close the door behind her. As she looked back, though, the door closed on its own. Her eyes widened, but she kept running.

What was happening? She didn't have time to guess. The pirates had already busted through the door and were continuing giving chase.

Ahead of her, another door opened. She ran through, and it shut behind her. Then another door opened, and it led outside. After she exited, the door shut again.

"Where's she at?" she heard.

"Wasn't that the cap's woman?" the other asked. They were still coming after her.

Across a small path, another door opened, and she ran through. Everywhere she turned, doors opened and closed of their own accord. She didn't know where they were leading her, but she had the feeling they were helping her escape.

Finally, she entered a room, but no other doors opened. She stood quiet and listened…but she didn't hear anything. She must have lost the pirates. But she couldn't stay here long. She needed to get to the boats. There were other doors to the room, but each one she tried was locked.

Why was I led here?

She looked around, and as her eyes adjusted, she realized she was in a library. The round room had ceilings at least ten feet high, and the wall was simply shelves of books. More books than she could even count.

While Catheryn could read, she never had much time for it as a slave. As much as she could recall, she'd never read a book for pleasure.

She continued walking around the room, trying the doors that occasionally broke up the shelves, when one book caught her eye. Why this one book out of the thousands drew her gaze, she had no idea, but she reached out and ran her fingers along the binding. She pulled the book down from its place on the shelf and looked at the cover.

The Power of Hoodoo it read.

"No way."

Maybe this book could help give her answers about what was happening.

"Thank you," she whispered, but she had no idea to whom. She put the book in her satchel and tried the next door. It opened right away. "Curiouser and curiouser," she mumbled.

As she exited the library, she realized she was on the edge of the town. She could see the bay in the distance. Excited, she ran for it. Her heart pumped in her chest. She was so close to freedom. To answers. Everything was going to be okay!

As she neared the boats, she suddenly ran smack into something. She fell backward and landed on her backside.

"Just where do you think you're going?" a voice asked her.

She looked up, and her eyes met Captain Rainier's.

CHAPTER 8

There were so many humans. More in one place than Captain Rainier had seen in...months? Years? It was amazing, human's tenacity for survival. No matter what they faced, be it natural disasters, supernatural curses, or the arrival of a far superior hunter, humans survived.

Rainier ordered his men to surround the village and pick off the outliers first, any guards or people foolish enough to be out so late at night. Then they snuck into the village itself. It wasn't long before they were spotted and someone raised the alarm. This did more to aid the vampires though than protect the humans. Out of fear, valor, or curiosity, many humans came out of the safety of their homes, allowing themselves to be picked off, to either be carried away for food or to be used as bait to draw out more humans.

In addition to human booty, the vampires also collected valuables and foodstuffs. Some of the vampires were so quick about their work, they were able to return to the lifeboats, take their prizes back to the ship, and then return to the shore for another run.

Rainier, even though he would have loved to have been part of the action, stayed near the lifeboats to direct his men and let them have their fun. He knew that some of the men were jealous that he had his own blood slave, so he wanted make sure the men enjoyed their time plundering the village. There would certainly be enough slaves collected to feed his men for months after this. That would go a long way toward boosting morale.

"Captain!" one of the men shouted as he ran toward him. It was Mathis, the first mate. "I saw her, sir," he said.

"Saw who?" Rainier asked.

"Your slave girl, Catheryn."

"What? Here? Are you sure?"

"I'm sure, captain," he said. "She was wearing the same clothes and had the same hair."

Rainier wondered just how Mathis knew what Catheryn had been wearing good enough to recognize in a fleeting moment in the dark of night, but he let the question linger for now.

"Where did she go?" he asked. "Why didn't you catch her?"

"That girl..." Mathis said, his voice ominous. "She's a witch, I tell you. She ran away quick like, but then she ran into a building, but she didn't open the door herself. One by one, the doors opened and closed on their own."

Rainier squinted his eyebrows. "You are sure she wasn't just opening them quickly? Or that someone else opened them, someone you couldn't see?"

"I'm certain she was alone, sir," he said. "What I saw...it weren't natural."

"Where is she now?" Rainier asked.

"I'm sorry to say I lost track of her, sir," he said. "But she was running through the village, from the far side to this way. She's probably thinking she can steal one of these here boats and make her escape."

Rainier nodded. "That makes sense," he said. "Good job warning me so I can be on the lookout. Now, get back to gathering that booty!"

"One more thing, sir," Mathis said. "Pardon if it's not my place. But if she's a witch, and she has been your personal blood slave... Have you been feeling all right, sir?"

"Right as rain," Rainier lied. Of course he has felt odd since he started feeding on Catheryn. But he couldn't let his men know that. He couldn't show any sign of weakness. "I'm sure she just... has a few tricks up her sleeve. You know how wily women are."

Mathis gave a lascivious laugh. "Don't I ever," he said in a way that even made Rainier's skin crawl.

"Back to work!" Rainier ordered.

"Aye-aye, sir!" Mathis said as he headed back toward the village.

Rainier shook his head as he thought about Catheryn. Damn that girl! Didn't she know how dangerous it could be out here without him as a protector? What if one of the other vampires caught her and didn't recognize her as his? She could be killed.

What if she was a witch, though? In that case, she could protect herself. But if she was, then why did she allow Rainier to take her captive, to feed off her? Why didn't the Hoodoo Queen protect her?

She couldn't actually be a witch...could she? Either way, she would certainly have a lot to answer for when he next saw her. Where was she anyway? Maybe he should go into the village and look for her...

As he debated what to do, he saw her. She was on the edge of the village, peeking toward the boats. Rainier had wandered away, pacing as he pondered what Mathis had told him, so she probably didn't see him. He let her make a break for it. She looked adorable as she pumped her arms, her black tresses bouncing behind her, trying so hard to make it to a boat unseen.

Foolish girl.

Just as she was about at the boats, Rainier used his preternatural speed to block her path. She ran into him with a thud and fell onto her backside.

"Just where do you think you're going?" he asked her.

She gasped. "C-C-Captain Rainier!"

"Obviously," he said. "Did you think you could get away from me so easily? And why would you want to get away? Have I not taken care of you? Fed you? Protected you? Even let you sleep in my own bed?"

She inched away from him as though afraid. But why? He had not been unkind to her.

"Where would you go? What would you do?" he asked even though she still had not answered his previous questions.

Still, she did not answer, but only backed farther away.

"What is wrong?" he asked. "Why won't you answer me?"

"Because you do not want to hear the truth," she said.

"What truth?" he asked. "That I saved you from slavery to the Hoodoo Queen? That I protected you from being drained by my starving crew? How could you be so ungrateful?"

Catheryn stood and faced Rainier. "You expect me to be grateful?" she asked. "For what? For being your dinner? For being threatened with chains if I displease you? For having to live my life in fear? Of pirates, of raiders, of *you*?"

Her words cut him deeply. She was afraid of him? But...why? And why should he care? She *should* fear him. She *should* only be food. She *should* be chained like the slave she was. Damnit! Why was he feeling sympathy for this troublesome girl?

"I have been good to you, Catheryn, in only the ways I know how," he said. "I am sorry if they are not the ways you are accustomed to or the ways you would like, but that is how it is. I am a vampire and you...well, I was going to say that you are a human, but that's not exactly true, is it?"

At that, her eyes widened, her fear returning. She turned and took flight once again.

"Catheryn!" he bellowed as he groaned and took off after her.

She was quick, but he was quicker. As she made her way back into the village, he saw what Mathis had described earlier. The doors ahead of her opened at will, and once she was safely through it, the door slammed shut. He couldn't tell if she was causing it, though, or if there was some other unseen force at play.

He burst through the first door, following her. He ducked as a vase flew toward him. He then had to dodge a book and a candlestick before Catheryn fled through another door. At the next building, though, he did not follow her through. He ran around the other side and was waiting as she exited. She practically ran into his arms. She struggled, kicked, and screamed, but he did not let her go.

"Calm yourself, Catheryn," he said. "I'm not going to hurt you."

"You're just going to take me back to your ship and feed on me," she said.

"I…" He sighed. "What else am I to do?" he asked. "Tell me, and I will do it. How will I survive if I do not feed on human blood?"

That gave her pause. Of course, she did not have an answer for him. Vampires had been trying to find an answer to that question for as long as they had existed and had not found a way around this problem. Many had tried to find a workaround. Some people had even tried to "cure" vampirism, as though it was some sort of disease. That was what had led to the great Rift in the first place. A vampire and a witch were trying to find a vampire cure and had fallen in love, their union shattering the entire world.

Most vampires, though, Rainier included, did not view vampirism as a disease to be cured. It was simply a new state of being that others would have to find a way to exist around.

"I suppose…if you must feed on someone," Catheryn said slowly, "it may as well be me."

He felt her tension in his arms melt away, and he loosened his grip. "That's more like it," he said. "So, uneasy truce, then?"

She nodded. "Uneasy truce."

He let her go and motioned back toward the lifeboats. She led the way back, but it appeared she was in no rush to return. He did not hurry her.

When they arrived back at the boats, most of them were full of pirates and their booty, both living and inanimate.

Mathis walked over to Rainier. "I see you found her, sir."

"Indeed I did," he said. "Has everyone returned?"

"Aye, sir," he said. "I think this should be our last haul. The humans are regrouping now and could fight back more effectively if we tried to attack again. But we have forty-seven humans at my last count, plus Miss Catheryn. Not to mention the rest of the booty. I think we should head back."

Rainier nodded. "Agreed. I'll take the last boat myself, along with Miss Catheryn."

"Aye, sir," Mathis said as he finished helping the other pirates load the boats, then they shoved off.

Rainier helped Catheryn into the last boat and then jumped in beside her. He rowed leisurely, taking in the night air. The moon was high and reflected off the ocean. The water lapped against the shore. There was the faint cry of wailing in the distance as people mourned the dead and the stolen. It was a magical evening.

He noticed Catheryn shudder a bit and pull her shawl around her shoulders.

"Are you cold?" he asked.

"Not particularly," she said. "Just...wondering what my life will be like now that I have resigned myself to being your...what was it? Bloodbag, I think one of your men called it."

He shrugged. "Vulgar term," he said. "It dehumanizes those we must feed upon. I realize some people find it easier to view humans that way. I mean, would you be able to eat chickens if they talked as you do? But still. There should be more honor in it than that."

Catheryn scoffed but didn't say anything.

"What?" he asked. "You think there can be no honor in staying alive?"

"I said nothing," she said. "This whole situation is far more complicated than I ever imagined."

"It is always easy for humans to think we are just a mindless evil when they have never had a conversation with us. Never considered that what we do is simply for survival. Same as they do."

"But you must understand their fear when you raid their village, steal their loved ones, and suck them dry and toss them into the sea," Catheryn said evenly, without malice, as though just stating the facts.

"I admit we have not come up with an…ideal way to coexist," he said.

"Would you change your ways?" she asked. "If someone found a way for you and humans to coexist in harmony?"

He did love being a vampire. The long life, superhuman strength, and bursts of speed. The feeling of being more powerful than any other living thing on earth. The freedom to roam the land and sea as he desired.

But what Catheryn had said earlier about the vampiric need for blood not being sustainable was true. He couldn't live without humans. They needed to find a way to coexist. Not just exist, but thrive. The world, or the division of NOLA at least, was dying. The waters were rising, crops were getting harder to grow, and the vampire numbers were dwindling. It was getting harder and harder to create vampires by turning a human. He could barely remember the last time it had happened successfully.

Finally, he nodded. "I would," he said. "We need to find a better way to exist."

"I might hold you to that," she said.

"Are you going to create this new world for me?" he asked with a chuckle.

"I just might," she said. "At least trying would give me something to fill my days while I am trapped in your quarters."

He smirked, raising one of his eyebrows. "Along with improving your magic?"

She blanched.

"I saw what was happening with the doors," he said. "The way they opened and closed on their own. Why have you been lying to me? Are you a witch or not?"

Catheryn sighed. "I don't know what I am. I never had powers growing up. They've only been manifesting recently. And only very small things anyway. I guess I could have had an ancestor who was a witch, so I could have a bit of witch blood in me. But my parents died when I was young. I don't even remember them. I was living on the street. Starving. Hiding in fear. I finally sold myself into slavery for...for just a bite to eat. Why would a witch be a slave? If I could have used powers to find another way, I would have. If I could have found a coven to take me in and train me, I would have.

"I have been suspecting for a while that I might be a lesser witch. Someone with latent magical powers that are of nearly no account. But I was already a slave in the Hoodoo House when I started noticing them. If the Hoodoo Queen had found out I was a witch, even a lesser one, and I didn't have a coven of my own to protect me..." She stopped and shuddered again.

Rainier nodded. "Things tend to only happen when you are threatened," he said. "Like the doors when you were chased or the beam when you were cornered."

"Yes," she said. "I noticed that as well. Which is why I think the powers are only latent. I cannot control them, but they take on a life of their own to protect me."

"Yet they allowed you to be captured by me," he said, wiggling his eyebrows. "Perhaps your powers knew I was not a threat to you."

"Or they just weren't quite strong enough yet to fight you off, but it's only a matter of time," she said with a teasing smirk.

"Well, we will have to see what other surprises you have in store for me, Catheryn Beauregard," he said.

He smiled as they rowed back to the ship. He wanted to believe what she had told him. He didn't have a reason not to believe her, except that she hadn't been completely honest with him before. More like lying by omission. But she didn't trust him before. Why should she? At least now they seemed to have turned a corner.

But the truth of what she was still gnawed at him. It should be safe for him to feed off a lesser witch. They were usually close enough to human that there should be no side effects from feeding off one. Yet every time he fed from Catheryn, he had those strange visions. And he wasn't feeling energized the way he should afterward.

There was still something about Catheryn that didn't make sense.

As they boarded the ship, Catheryn headed straight to their...*his* quarters. He couldn't help but notice the other crewmen watching her as she passed. She was a beautiful woman, and it made him proud to call her his. But he noticed that Mathis's gaze lingered a little longer than it should.

Rainier didn't like that at all.

atheryn...

"Rainier?" Catheryn called out. She opened her eyes and looked around, but she was alone. Funny. She could have sworn she heard someone say her name. She must have been in that place between sleep and awake, that place where you can't tell dreams from reality.

She sat up in the bed and stretched. She had to admit, she could get used to sleeping in her own comfy bed and waking when she wanted to.

Okay, it was Rainier's bed, and he had slept in it, too. But he hadn't tried anything. They had both been so exhausted when they finally returned they just collapsed into bed and fell asleep. Since she was going to be Rainier's kept woman for a while, maybe she could talk to him about getting her a bed of her own. At least a mattress on the floor instead of a pile of straw would be nice, and more appropriate.

She walked over to the door and looked through the glass. She could once again see the men working, going about their business. She saw Rainier, too, but he didn't seem to see her. He was too busy giving orders and keeping an eye on everything.

If only he wasn't a vampire.

What? He'd still be a pirate. Actually, no, he wouldn't. There were no human pirates. They'd all been killed or ran aground long ago. It was simply too dangerous for them. They couldn't compete with the vampires.

Catheryn shook her head and went to Rainier's desk where her usual bowl of grits with honey and a glass of orange juice were waiting for her. Today, there was also a fresh fluffy biscuit. The cook must have been taking advantage of the provisions they had secured last night.

Stole! she reminded herself. They *stole* those goods, and those people. Those poor people. Trapped below deck. Scared out of their minds. She shuddered. Maybe there wasn't anything she could do for them, but at least she could be honest with herself about the reality of their situation.

Catheryn...

She heard something in the back of her mind. Not a voice really, but something like a memory, clawing at her, trying to get her attention. As she finished her breakfast, she looked around, hoping she would see something that would jar her memory. Then she saw her bag.

The book!

She had forgotten all about it when she arrived back at the ship. She pulled the book from her bag, took it over to the desk, and admired the artisanship in the light. It was large and bound in dark, nearly black leather. The title of the book and the skull and what looked like runes on the front were gold embossed.

She opened the book carefully and ran her fingers over the pages, which were no ordinary paper, but vellum. Each letter— each embellishment—had been meticulously drawn.

The book seemed to be a mix of folk tales and folk magic, telling stories of why hoodoo was used, who used it, and how. She read one story of how an old woman used her connections to the earth to help plants germinate and grow. Another story was about a father who loved his children so much that, when he died, he poured out his essence so that he could protect them throughout the generations. The stories were beautiful, romantic, and heartbreaking. But the one theme that ran through them all was that they were good. The people and their motives for using the hoodoo were pure of spirit.

She thought about her experiences with hoodoo before this moment. Nearly everything she knew about hoodoo came from what she had seen in the Hoodoo House, under the control of the Hoodoo Queen.

In the Hoodoo House, indeed throughout most of the NOLA Division, the Hoodoo Queen was a woman to be feared. She used her powers to control the division's resources and elevate her status. It was her dream that NOLA would eventually be her personal domain.

The Hoodoo Queen's use of magic was almost completely selfish, and certainly terrifying. But according to this book, hoodoo was primarily used for good, and for selfless reasons.

Catheryn decided to try a simple spell, just to test the veracity of the book and her own abilities. She found a spell for making an amulet of protection. She certainly thought that would be useful, living on a vampire pirate ship.

Almost everything she needed she was able to find in Rainier's quarters: a small leather bag, a string of horsehair, two gold coins, and water. The last item she needed, though, was a pinch of salt. Salt, like most spices, was a precious commodity. She would have to try to find some in the ship's kitchen.

She took her empty food tray with her and headed below deck. That ought to be a good excuse to go down there. The kitchen was on the second deck. Surprisingly, she didn't see any of the humans who had been captured the night before. They were probably being kept in the very lowest deck, below sea level, trapped in cages. She shuddered. She would have to find a way to help them.

When she found the kitchen, the cook was scurrying around. He was a short, plump man with a friendly face. She had seen him before, when he would bring her her meals, but they had never spoken.

"You didn't have to do that, missy," he said, taking her tray. "I could have picked it up when I brought you your lunch."

"I don't mind," she said. "I really just wanted an excuse to get out of the cabin, stretch my legs a bit," Catheryn said, her eyes darting around the room, trying to figure out where the salt might be kept.

"It's no mind, no mind," the cook said. "Is there anything else ye be needin'? We got a good haul last night, as I'm sure you know."

"The biscuit was a nice treat this morning," she said.

"Oh, aye!" the cook replied, beaming. "Glad you noticed. Nothin' beats grams' homemade biscuits."

"Is that who you learned to cook from? Your gram?" Catheryn asked, making polite conversation.

"Oh, yes," the cook said, a wistful gleam in his eye. "Not the same, though. Hard to find some of the ingredients she used. She made everything with a big spoonful of butter, and that was many, many lifetimes ago. Hard to keep butter on a ship like this these days."

"I'm sure," Catheryn said. "You make due pretty well, though. I certainly love the little dollop of honey on the grits. Your grandmother must have been a southerner."

The cook laughed as he opened a pantry and pulled out some ingredients. Catheryn noticed several small bags. *Spices!*

"Oh, that she was," the cook said with a laugh, but Catheryn had forgotten what she said to illicit that response. She had to create a distraction so she could find the salt.

She spied a crate of oranges. She concentrated and willed the crate to tip over. But nothing happened. She sighed and thought about what Rainier had said about her powers manifesting when she was in danger. She certainly wasn't in danger now, talking to this kindly cook. She had to find another way to distract him.

"Well, why I don't I help you with these dishes," she said as she moved toward a tub on the countertop that served as a sink.

"Oh, that's not necessary, dearie," he said as he reached for the tray.

Catheryn just happened to let go of the tray before he could grab it, and the whole lot crashed to the floor.

"Oh no! I'm so clumsy!" Catheryn exclaimed. "I'm so sorry. Let me help you clean it up."

"No mind," the cook said. "Don't cut yourself. You don't want to find yourself bleeding on a ship of vampires. Just let me get the broom."

When he left to go around the corner, Catheryn opened the pantry and stuck her fingers in every bag, using touch to try to find the salt. She didn't have much time; who knew how quickly he'd return. She felt the texture of the contents of each bag, guessing which each was: flour, sugar, something leafy...and then, there it was. Salt! She grabbed a handful, stuffed it into her pocket, and closed the door to the pantry just before the cook came back.

"You best step back," he reiterated as he came back. "Even though everyone has eaten their fill lately, some vampires imply cannot resist the smell of fresh blood."

Even though Catheryn thought he was just giving a polite warning, she couldn't help feeling a sense of unease creep over her. The cook seemed like a nice, safe man...but he was a vampire, too. All vampires had a base, animalistic nature. She should never get too comfortable around any of them. They could always turn on you in a shot.

She nodded as she headed out. "I'm really sorry," she said. "But thank you again for the lovely breakfast and good conversation."

"Feel free to come down and see me anytime," he said as he waved her away and crouched down to clean up the mess.

Catheryn practically flew back to her room and shut the door.

She ran back to the desk and followed the instructions to construct the amulet. She placed the coins and salt inside the bag. She used the horsehair string to tie the bag shut and create a loop so she could wear it around her neck. The only part she wasn't sure about was where it said to "carve a rune of your soul on the bag."

What on the great seas did that mean? She flipped through the book, but could find no information about what a rune of your soul was. She finally decided that it must be something personal, something unique to each person.

Using a letter opener, she etched a symbol into the leather of the bag. She didn't know what it was supposed to be. It swirled to the right, the left, and the right again, and she placed two dots inside two of the swirls. Hopefully it would be good enough. She placed her newly crafted amulet around her neck and recited the casting that had to accompany it.

Night and Shade
Daylight Fade
Protect the light
That burns inside

She waited, but nothing happened. She didn't know what she expected, but perhaps the magic was more passive, more like a good luck charm. She shrugged and started to clean up the little mess she made and was looking for somewhere to hide the book when she heard a slow creaking sound behind her. The little hairs of warning perked up on the back of her neck, and she thought she felt a warming in her chest where the amulet was hanging. She turned and saw Mathis, the first mate.

"You've been a bad girl," Mathis said, licking his lips.

"What are you talking about?" she asked.

"I saw you, in the kitchen, sweet talking ol' Cook. I saw what you did."

Her face went hot. Had he seen her steal the salt? Or was he just bluffing? She didn't know, but she knew that he was bad news. She had seen the way he eyed her. And the fact that the amulet was growing hot on her chest told her that the spirits knew he was dangerous, too.

"You can't...you can't be here," she said. "This is Rainier's room. He won't like that you're here."

"He's a bit busy at the moment," he said, motioning to the large window at the back of the room.

She backed up to the window, sure to not turn her back on Mathis. She looked out the window and saw Rainier and a couple of his men in a lifeboat being pulled behind *The Dark Storm*.

"What's he doing out there?" she asked.

"Just assessing some damage from the fight before," he said. "But he'll be out there a while. Long enough, anyway."

Catheryn swallowed. "Long enough for what?"

"I think you know," he said as he stepped toward her.

She stepped away and held her hand out. "You better leave me alone," she said. "I'm Captain Rainier's private property. If you touch me, he'll know, and he won't be pleased."

"You just let me worry about Rainier," he said as he stepped toward her again, quickly this time. "You should worry about yourself."

"Believe me, I am," she said as she backed away, pulling a chair between them.

She didn't know what to do. Rainier was too far away. She couldn't control her powers. She didn't know how the amulet worked. It was warm, but did it do anything else? Would it actually keep him away? Amplify her powers so she could protect herself? She didn't know anything about actually using magic. She needed more time to study the book.

Mathis laughed. "That's not exactly what I mean. I saw you, in the kitchen, using your wily woman ways on the old cook."

Catheryn swallowed.

"I saw you stealing," he said. "Salt is a precious commodity. Worth more than the likes of you. If the captain found out, he wouldn't have a choice but to punish you. Maybe chop off your hand. Maybe hand you over to the rest of the crew..." He licked his lips. "But, if you were to come over here, maybe sit on my lap, maybe I could find it in my heart to not say anything."

She backed away again.

"Stay back!" she said, more firmly this time.

Her heart raced. He had seen her stealing. She flashed back to the Hoodoo House and the witch who had caught her stealing there, too. She'd nearly killed the woman. Would she have to do that again?

"I'm warning you," she said, her confidence wavering a bit.

Mathis guffawed. "Warning me? You are a daft girl. Good thing you have one fine ass..." He licked his lips again and lunged toward her.

She turned to run but ran into a dresser. She pivoted around it, but in that split moment, Mathis had gained ground on her. He reached out and grabbed her wrist. She spun around to slap him, but he grabbed her other wrist as well.

"Let me go!" she screamed.

The amulet grew hot—so hot it might burn.

"Don't fight it, bitch," he snapped as he reached for her skirt.

"Help me!" she screamed. "Help!"

But there was no magic to save her.

CHAPTER 10

Rainier had felt something was wrong, and as he burst through the door to his quarters, his suspicions were confirmed.

He narrowed his gaze as Mathis to loosened his grip on Catheryn.

"What is the meaning of this?" Rainier asked. "Why are you in my quarters?"

Of course, it was obvious what Mathis was doing. But Rainier wanted to give him a chance to redeem himself. The two had been together for...decades...and Mathis had always been a reliable first mate and friend. But he had seen the way Mathis had been eying Catheryn.

Mathis let go of Catheryn and gave a quick salute. "Cap'n, sir," he said. "This girl ain't good for you."

Catheryn ran away from Mathis and stood by the bed.

"What do you mean?" Rainier asked.

"She's trouble. I saw her stealing salt from the kitchen."

Rainier looked at Catheryn. "Is this true?"

She didn't answer, but her eyes were pleading.

"You'll have to punish her, sir," Mathis said. "I think..."

"You are dismissed," Rainier said.

"...Sir?" Mathis asked, stumbling over his words.

"Leave, now," Rainier said. "You overstep your bounds. I thank you for telling me about the girl's crime, but you'll not tell me how to act as captain. Is that understood?"

"Aye, sir," Mathis said, deflation in his voice. His shoulders drooped as he headed toward the door.

"And, Mathis," Rainier continued, "if I find you in my quarters again, or see you touching my property, I'll chop off your hand. Have I made myself clear?"

Mathis didn't look back at him, but it sounded as though he was responding through gritted teeth when he said, "Yes, sir." Then he quickly exited through the door.

Catheryn audibly sighed.

"Did he hurt you?" Rainier asked.

"No," she replied.

"Do you think he was going to?" he asked. "Were you in danger?"

"I'm certain he was going to...assault me," she said.

"You didn't use you powers on him?" he asked. "You are usually better at defending yourself."

"I think..." She swallowed on a lump forming in her throat. "How did you get here so quickly? I saw you, through the window, in the boat observing the damage to the ship."

He nodded. "We can move at an uncanny pace if we so desire," he explained. "I had a feeling something was wrong, that you were in danger. I had to come back and check on you. It was as though an alarm was going off in my head, and it wouldn't stop until I knew you were safe."

"I think it was my powers," she said. "I don't know why they called out to you instead of helping me protect myself like before, but I don't pretend to know anything about the ways of hoodoo just yet."

"Just yet?" he asked. "Are you learning?"

Catheryn blanched and gave a small nod. Rainier felt the edge of his lip try to turn up in a smile. She was so cute when she was trying to hide things from him. He then noticed she was wearing something like a necklace.

"What is that bag around your neck?" he asked. "I didn't notice you wearing any jewelry before."

She reached up and touched the bag. "Oh, it's not jewelry. It's a charm I made. A protection spell of sorts."

"Did it work?" he asked, taking a few steps forward to get a better look.

"I think it called to you," she said. "It grew hot when Mathis threatened me, and then you showed up at just the right moment."

Rainier felt himself puff up with pride a bit at that. He wasn't used to being considered a hero.

"How did you know to make it?" he asked.

She lowered her head, once again not wanting to tell him the truth. "I...I found something...in the village. A book."

"A book?" he asked.

She nodded. "Yes, a book about hoodoo magic."

"Show me," he said.

She walked over to the desk where the book was lying open. She must have been reading it when Mathis came in.

"While I was in the village, I came across a huge library," she said. "There were thousands of books. But this one...this one seemed to call out to me. I just had to take it."

Rainier turned the book toward him and flipped some of the pages. He couldn't make sense of it.

"You can read this?" he asked.

Catheryn nodded, her brow knitted above her hooded eyes.

"This doesn't make any sense to me," he said. "It's just scribbles and lines."

"What does that mean?" she asked.

Rainier shrugged. "It must be enchanted in some way. Did you use any kind of spell to open it or translate it?"

"No," Catheryn said. "I just opened it and read it like any book. I mean, I know it isn't just any book, but I didn't have to do anything special to start reading it."

"So the question is," Rainier said, "is the book only meant for you to read, or could any witch read it?"

"Or maybe it is enchanted to prevent vampires from reading it," Catheryn offered, a small smile on her lips.

Rainier chuckled. "Cleaver girl. That's an option, too."

They smiled at each other, and Rainier felt something pass between them. An affability, a comradery that wasn't there before. There was a comfort, an easy way of talking as though they were two friends sharing in this great discovery. Rainier felt as if he should say something, do something, but he wasn't sure what. Should he touch her? Kiss her? That seemed like too much too quickly, but he felt as if the moment should be celebrated in some way.

Catheryn cleared her throat and looked away, and the moment passed. Rainier took another look at the charm around her neck. The symbol on it, he was sure he had seen it before.

"That symbol on the bag around your neck, it wasn't there before, was it?" he asked.

"No," she said. "I drew it."

"Did the book tell you to draw it?"

"Not exactly," she said. "The instructions said to 'carve a rune of your soul on the bag.' I couldn't find an example of a rune of your soul in the book, so I figured it must be something personal. So I just carved whatever seemed to come naturally."

"Do you know what it is?" he asked.

"No," she said, looking at it. "Just some swirls. Why?"

"Because I've seen that symbol before," he said.

"What?" Catheryn asked, eyes wide. "Where?"

"I can't remember exactly where I saw it," he said. "If it was in a book or...somewhere else. But I know I've seen it. We vampires, we are not witches, but some very powerful, very old vampires have some access to the magical realm. And some of them remember the time before the Rift, a time when vampires and witches sometimes worked together and formed alliances. So we vampires have some knowledge of spirit lore."

"And...?" Catheryn prodded.

"And I am sure that rune is the symbol of a powerful pure blood hoodoo witch family."

Catheryn took a step back, her eyes darting wildly. "But...but what does that mean?" she asked. "I had never seen it before that I remember, not even in the hoodoo house. I thought it was something unique, something original. Why would this rune come to my mind?"

"Why did the book speak to you?" Rainier asked.

"I don't know!" Catheryn cried, wringing her hands.

"Do you remember your parents at all?" Rainier asked. "Your family?"

Catheryn shook her head. "They died when I was little. My sister and I—we were on our own. But what does this mean? Why would I...know this? And why is this happening now? I've been a slave in the Hoodoo House for years and things only started happening recently. What is happening with me?"

Rainier paced the cabin and ran his fingers through his hair in frustration. He didn't know. He couldn't think. It seemed as though the answer was near to him, just beyond his grasp. As though he should know the answer, but he couldn't see it in the dark.

He needed to feed. He hadn't had a good feed since he brought Catheryn on board. Every time he fed from her, he felt weaker after, not stronger. And those strange visions he would get. What was happening to *him*?

Feeding from Catheryn had been pleasurable, but not satisfying. He was still left hungry, which was making him grumpy and leaving his brain in a fog.

He knew, logically, that he should probably feed from

someone else. They had a large store of humans now. He could simply feed from any of them and be restored. Yet, to do that felt...wrong somehow. He knew Catheryn wouldn't like it, and that bothered him far more than it should. He shouldn't feel beholden to some human. Some witch. He worthless bloodbag. But he couldn't shake the growing affection he was feeling for her. And she had finally submitted to serving as his devotee. He couldn't very well go feed on someone else now.

"Catheryn," he said gently. "I must feed. I have not eaten since yesterday. I cannot function if I do not feed."

He looked at her and knew there was hunger in his eyes. He only hoped that his hunger looked more akin to desire than like a hungry dog staring at a piece of meat. He didn't want to scare her.

He could almost hear her heart rate increase. He saw her breath hitch and her eyes widen. She blushed and color rushed to her cheeks. She wanted him to feed on her.

He felt what little blood he had rush to his groin. His desire to feed was shared by his desire to hold her in his arms, feel his lips on her neck, run his fingers over her body.

The vampire's embrace was pleasurable for both parties. It was not uncommon for a feeding to turn into a...more intimate encounter. He wondered if Catheryn would be willing to take their relationship to that level.

He held out his hand, and she took it. He pulled her to him. He could tell that she was nervous, but she pulled her hair back and tilted her neck to him. He lowered his mouth to her neck, but he didn't bite her yet. He ran his nose over her skin and breathed in deeply. She sighed.

"Is this all you want, Catheryn?" he asked. "Just for me to bite you and be done with it?"

"What more is there?" she asked breathlessly.

He lightly kissed her neck and placed his hands on her waist, pressing his body against hers. "There is so much more," he whispered.

She whimpered. "But...you're a vampire," she said. "I...we don't know what I am, but I am at least a lesser witch. We...we can't...it's forbidden..."

"Who would know all the way out here?" he asked, placing delicate kisses along her neck and then reaching up and squeezing her breast.

She gasped and placed her arm around him, holding him close, willing him on. Her actions were warring with her words. Her desire fighting with her reason. "It's dangerous," she said. "A vampire and a witch were together only once before...and they shattered the world."

He placed his lips on hers and kissed her deeply. She kissed him back, leaning into him, opening her mouth and welcoming him inside.

"I'm a pirate," he said. "I live for danger. Let this crummy world shatter again for all I care."

At that, he picked her up and tossed her onto the bed. He undid his belt, letting his holster and scabbard clatter to the floor. He tossed aside his hat and his heavy coat. He leaped on top of her and kissed her lips, her cheeks, her neck.

She pulled up her skirt and ran her fingers along his back, holding him close.

His fangs descended. He had to feed before they could make love. He wouldn't have enough energy or blood of his own to actually take her if he didn't.

He bit into her neck, and she cried out—first in pain, then in pleasure. He drank from her, taking her warmth into him. She was delicious, and he started to feel energized. Maybe the feedings before were just flukes, strange reactions to her new blood and because he had not fed in so long before he brought her on board.

As he fed, he ran his hands down her legs and placed himself between her thighs. He was going to take her as soon as he had eaten his fill. She was already panting and moaning. She was ready for him.

Then he saw the sparks.

He looked up and saw a woman. At first he thought it was Catheryn, but then he realized it wasn't. This woman was younger with short hair. She was leading an attack on the Hoodoo House. There was fire everywhere. The house was burning to the ground...

His eyes shot open, and he stopped the feeding.

"Rainier?"

He heard Catheryn's voice, but it sounded...muddled. As if she was far away.

Rainier shook his head and sat up. Then the world went black.

CHAPTER 11

As Rainier fell backward, Catheryn summoned what little strength she had to grab him and help him fall forward on the bed instead of to the floor. She felt exhausted as well and curled up beside him. While she was a bit disappointed he had fallen asleep, she was grateful as well. What was this man doing to her? Did she really want to make love to a vampire? Was she crazy? He was an undead monster. She needed to be more careful. She couldn't let him get too close. Especially since they didn't know what she was.

She warred with the thoughts in her mind and eventually drifted off to sleep.

The next morning, she once again woke up alone. Her breakfast was waiting for her, as usual. After she ate, she looked out the window and thought she saw land in the distance. Excited, she left the cabin and ran up to the helm.

"Where are we going?" she asked Rainier. "Is that land in the distance?"

Rainier cocked an eyebrow. "You have good eyes," he said. "We might have to station you up in the crow's nest."

He nodded to the helmsman, dismissing him so he and Catheryn were alone at the ship's wheel. Rainier steered the ship with ease.

He took in a deep breath and then slowly let it out. "Can you smell the sea?"

Catheryn took in the salty air. "Salt. Water. Fish," she said.

"Freedom," he said. "Adventure. Danger. Treasure. Fame. I smell all that and more. This is what it means to me, being a pirate on the dark seas. There is no other life for me. Do you understand?"

Catheryn shook her head. "Not really. It's not that I'm not sympathetic," she clarified. "I think it's wonderful you love what you do. But I've never experienced that. I've always been a slave. Well, before that I was a beggar. I've never had a job or work that I loved or even chose to do."

Rainier nodded. "Well, one day you will find your calling. For me, the sea sings to me. There is nothing else I could do. Nothing I would want to do. If I was forced to live on the land, I swear I would dry up and die."

"What are you even talking about?" Catheryn asked. "Who's forcing you to give up a life you love?"

"You are," he said pointedly.

Catheryn took a step back. "Me? What are you talking about?"

He sighed and looked out over the helm for a moment before continuing, as though he was unsure how to continue.

"You are not what you claim to be, Catheryn," he said. She opened her mouth to protest, but he held up his hand. "I do not think you are lying to me, not knowingly at least. I believe you when you say your powers only started recently and are weak. I believe you when you say you don't know anything about your past. But I think you are far more powerful than you know. That you are becoming...something else."

Catheryn felt her heart beat fast. Her head started to spin. A part of her knew he was right. She could feel it, this power growing inside her. She wanted to ignore it, tamp it down. Even though her abilities thrilled her in the moment, they terrified her upon reflection. What if she didn't like what she was turning into? What if she couldn't control it?

"But...but how do you know this?" Catheryn asked.

"Because when I feed from you, you are draining my vampirism from me," he said. He looked her straight in the eyes when he said it, and she felt her blood run cold.

"I don't...I don't understand," she said.

"I noticed it the first time I fed on you, but I didn't want to believe it," he explained. "I don't feel full from drinking your blood. I feel weaker afterward. But I don't just feel tired. I feel less...vampire. I desire blood less. I cannot move as quickly. I don't feel as strong."

"You still seem strong to me," Catheryn said.

Rainier chuckled. "Well, even as a mortal man, I would be an impressive specimen. Probably much stronger and larger than the average man." The smile crept away from his face. "But I will not be enough to survive as a pirate. A human pirate cannot compete with the vampire ships. Humans are weaker than vampires. There is no question. There hasn't been a human pirate ship in decades. The vampires simply killed them all or ran them aground. If I was no longer a vampire, I couldn't live on the sea, either."

"Then...you have to stop feeding from me," Catheryn said. "You'll have to feed from one of the other humans you captured."

"Perhaps," Rainier said. "But that won't answer the question of what you are."

"Does it matter?" Catheryn asked.

"Oh, yes, it certainly does," Rainier said. "Only someone very, very powerful could have this effect on a vampire. You know your power is growing. Whatever you are turning into, I'd like to have you by my side. Have you as an ally, not an enemy."

Catheryn paused. Was Rainier afraid of her? Afraid of what she was becoming? Afraid she might take her revenge on him when she came into her own? It sure sounded like it. Did he need to be afraid of her? If she did come into awe-inspiring power, would she turn on him? Would she have a choice?

A part of her was afraid of what she was becoming as well. What if she couldn't control it? Well, it didn't seem to matter. She was growing stronger, and she would have to do her best to grow along with it. Learn to control it. To for once be the master of her own fate.

"So, do you have a plan for finding out more about what I am?" she asked.

Rainier smiled and pointed to the island that was now clearly in view.

"Land ho!" he called loudly.

~

All of the pirates were anxious to get on land. They had only been on land for raids recently and had not been on land for pleasure or to even stretch their legs in quite a long time, it seemed. The men prepared the lifeboats to go ashore, along with any supplies they might need—ropes, shovels, sacks, and the like. They were supposed to have been heading for Revenge Bay, but Rainier had persuaded the men to travel to this remote place instead.

"What are your orders, cap'n?" Mathis asked once the men were ready and assembled on deck.

"Find treasure!" Rainier yelled, eliciting a round of cheers from the men. "According to this map we found in the village," he said, holding up a tattered bit of parchment, "there is treasure hidden here on the island. I am ordering you to find it."

The men cheered again.

"Mr. Mathis will lead the expedition," Rainier explained. "I will stay here to protect the ship. But you better not come back without the booty!"

"Let's go, men!" Mathis ordered. The men divided up into teams and got in their respective boats. "Are you sure about this, cap'n?" Mathis asked as he approached to take the map from Rainier. "You don't want to take part?"

"The men deserve a reward," Rainier said. "They have been working hard and have endured much. The bounty can be divided equally between them. They've earned it."

Catheryn sensed that Mathis didn't quite believe Rainier. That he thought Rainier was hiding something from him. Unfortunately, he was right, but he wasn't about to question his captain, not after the incident in Rainier's quarters.

After the men were all a safe distance away, rowing to the shore, Catheryn asked, "So where did you get that map?"

"I made it while you were sleeping," he said.

"Will they be mad if they don't find anything?" she asked.

Rainier shrugged. "Hopefully just at those lying villagers."

Catheryn didn't much like that. What if they decided to take out their anger on the poor villagers they had trapped below deck? She sighed. There wasn't anything she could do about that right now.

"So what is the plan?" she asked. "What are we really doing here?"

Rainier led her to the last remaining lifeboat and helped her in. "We are going to find answers."

Rainier and Catheryn pulled their boat ashore farther down the coast than the other pirates and behind a small group of rocks.

"Why are you hiding from your own men?" Catheryn asked. "They are your crew. They would help you find whatever you are looking for if you ordered them to, right?"

Rainier drew his cutlass as they headed into the jungle. "I am their captain, and they are my men. I give orders, yes, but they are not slaves. They work for me. It is my job to lead them, not drag them around by their ears. Sure, sometimes I must be firm with them, but there must be order for the ship to run smoothly.

"This is a personal quest," he continued. "One to find out what you are. That wouldn't benefit the men at all. They would resent me using them for personal gain."

"So what are we looking for?" she asked.

"A ship," he said. "A slave ship."

Catheryn stopped. "A slave ship? But…why?"

Rainier reached out for her hand. "That's why I didn't tell you before. I thought you might not want to come, what with your history."

"You got that for damn sure," Catheryn said, taking his hand roughly but letting him lead her along.

"Legend has it that this ship is special. It was once used to transport African slaves who happened to be a pure family of hoodoo witches," Rainier explained.

"If they were so powerful, how come they were slaves?" Catheryn grumbled.

"Maybe we will find out when we get there," Rainier said.

They walked along through the lush jungle with Rainier using his cutlass to forge their path.

"So how did you find yourself in slavery?" Rainier asked. "Were you born into it?"

"No," Catheryn said. "As I said, my parents died when I was young. I don't even remember them. My sister and I lived on the streets mostly. Begging and scrounging. One day, I messed up and we got caught."

Catheryn couldn't help but laugh a bit at that. Every time she stole something, it went badly for her. She should really stop thinking that thieving could solve her problems.

"What is it?" Rainier asked.

"Oh, nothing," Catheryn said, not wanting to tell him about the witch she almost killed in the Hoodoo House when she was trying to steal food. "Anyway, the man who caught us, he wanted us locked away, which is a fate worse than death for two little girls. So I volunteered to be a slave, to let the man sell me, if he let my sister go. So that's what happened. He took me up on the slaver's block, and I was bought by the Hoodoo Queen. I never saw my sister again."

"How long ago was that?" Rainier asked.

"Oh, I don't know," Catheryn said. "Fifteen, sixteen years ago? One day is pretty much like the next for a slave."

Rainier nodded. "I'm sorry," he said.

"At least being a slave for you has been a bit more exciting," Catheryn said.

Rainier went quiet. She wondered what he was thinking. He was probably still a bit worried about what would happen as her powers grew. He wouldn't be able to keep her as a slave for much longer, she reckoned, considering how much her powers had improved in the last few days alone.

What would she do then? Would she stay with Rainier? What else would she do? She didn't have a home to return to. She would need to find a coven of her own, but she had no idea how. She didn't really know how all the politics of being a witch worked.

Finally, the brush cleared. They had made their way to the other side of the island. And there before them, on the beach, was a wrecked ship.

Catheryn felt her heart beat hard in her chest. She wasn't sure why, but she felt a sudden surge of emotion at seeing the old decrepit beast before them.

The ship was nearly black with rot and age. About a third of it was buried in the sand. There were a few tattered rags of sails still waving in the wind.

"They say the ship is quite old," Rainier said, breaking into her thoughts. "From long before the Rift. Back when slaves were still brought over from Africa."

"You're talking hundreds of years," Catheryn said. Today, Africa was part of Devil's Bay division and there was no way to get there from NOLA. The magical shields that were stitching the world together were dividing them. "What happened to the slaves?"

Rainier made his way down toward the ship. "Well, if they survived the wreck, and I think they did, at least some of them, maybe the lifeboats were not damaged. They could have used them to sail away. We are not far from Haiti now. They could have made it there."

When she was younger, people often told her she had a Haitian accent. She wasn't sure what they were talking about since she didn't remember ever living anywhere but NOLA, but over time, her accent faded and now she sounded like anyone else.

Rainier kept talking as they worked their way closer to the ship. "Hoodoo magic originated in Africa. It made its way to the Americas when the Africans were brought here as slaves. Maybe your ancestors made it to Haiti and then later moved to North America."

Catheryn shrugged. "Maybe."

There was no real way to ever learn about her past. She was apprehensive about entering the ship. Maybe she didn't want to know what was in there. Maybe it would just make her life even more difficult. She was already scared of her powers growing on their own. She didn't think she was ready to learn whatever answers the ship might hold for her.

Rainier seemed to sense her unease. He held out his hand to her again. "Don't worry," he said. "I'm here. We will find the answers together."

There was a large hole in the ship that they could easily crawl through to get inside the lower decks. As Rainier grabbed hold of one of the boards to hoist himself up, eight giant eyes, each as big as Rainier's head, appeared before him. Rainier yelled and fell back.

Catheryn froze in fear as a monstrous spider crawled out of the ship and darted toward her.

CHAPTER 12

The great beast lunged out of the ship. Rainier dove out of the way as the massive creature stepped over him and ran toward Catheryn. Rainier drew his cutlass and yelled at the beast.

"Hey! Monster!" he called "Over here!"

The spider was at least ten feet tall, dark gray, with long hairy legs. It turned toward Rainier, and he almost swore it snarled at him, if a giant spider was capable of such a thing.

"Yes!" Rainier taunted. "You see me, don't you, you ugly bastard! Come at me!"

The head of the lumbering creature seemed to bounce, as though it was laughing at him! While Rainier stood there confused, the spider shot a wad of webbing from its spinnerets. Before he could think, he felt himself fly backward until he slammed against the hull of the wrecked ship. The webbing held him to the ship like glue. He struggled but could not pull himself free. His eyes darted around. He had dropped his sword. And then, he was hit by the spider's silk.

The spider then turned away from Rainier and set its eight eyes on Catheryn.

"Run!" Rainier yelled, even though he knew it was pointless. The spider was so huge it would overtake her in only a couple of steps. She could never hope to outrun it.

Catheryn seemed to realize the same thing, because she did not attempt to flee. The spider also appeared to be in no hurry since his quarry would not be able to escape. Catheryn took a step back, and Rainier saw her mouth move, as if she was mumbling something. Then she waved her arms in the air and small balls of fire appeared in each one.

At this, the spider grew angry. It let out something like a shriek as it charged at Catheryn. Even though Rainier knew he was helpless, he struggled against his bonds, desperate to help her.

But she didn't need his help. As the spider charged at her, she threw one of the balls of fire into the spider's eyes. The spider screamed, and Catheryn was able to jump out of its way as it continued running blindly. When she was clear of the spider, she rubbed her hands together, making the fireball she still held even bigger. She held the fireball in front of her and blew on it, and the fireball flew at the spider, hitting it in the rear of its abdomen. The spider let out a deafening cry of pain as it ran off into the jungle. Rainier had a feeling he wouldn't see the spider again.

Catheryn ran over to Rainier. "Are you hurt?"

"No, I'm fine," he said. "Grab my sword. Cut me down."

"Oh, right!" she said. She found the cutlass and used it to cut through the sticky webbing. "Have you ever seen such a monster before?" she asked. She didn't seem scared, but exhilarated.

"You wouldn't believe the things I've seen in my years at sea," he said.

As Catheryn cut the last sinew of the webbing, Rainier dropped safely and unharmed into the sand. They both looked at each other and laughed, both excited and relieved to be alive.

Rainier took Catheryn into his arms and kissed her. She kissed him back. He ran his fingers down her neck and her arms while she caressed his cheek.

"You saved me," he whispered. "I haven't been rescued by someone else since I was a boy."

"I don't think I've ever saved someone else's life before," Catheryn said. "I feel so...strong. Like I can do anything."

"If you can do anything," Rainier asked between kisses, "what do you *want* to do?"

He knew what *he* wanted to do. He wanted to throw her down and make love to her right there in the sand and surf. He could taste the anticipation on her tongue, her lips. He knew she felt the same way.

"I want..." She moaned. "I want..." She forced herself to pull away from him. "I want to find out what I am. Who I am. What is on this ship."

He cocked an eyebrow at her. "Are you sure?"

She nodded. "It...it's for the best. You know that."

Rainier sighed and cleared his throat as he reached down to his groin to adjust his deflating manhood. "Right. Sure. Let's explore this ship."

They both walked to the hole in the hull and looked inside.

"Are you sure there aren't any more spiders?" Catheryn asked.

"I'm not sure at all," he said. "But there is only one way to find out." Rainier climbed into the ship. "Hello!" he called out. "Any more spiders in here?"

The only reply was the lapping of waves on the shore and a few seagulls cawing nearby.

"I think it is safe," he said as he reached back to help Catheryn into the ship.

The inside of the ship was tilted since part of it was submerged in the sand, so it wasn't easy walking along the inside. But as they got their bearings and their eyes adjusted to the dark, it got a little easier. There were holes all along the hull, which let in more light the farther in they went.

"What...what part of the ship is this?" Catheryn asked.

Rainier looked around. "The cargo hold," he said. "At one time, these shelves were used to store goods. But..." He paused, unsure of just how much she wanted to know.

"But what?" she prodded. Still he hesitated. "Tell me."

"They have been converted into racks for people to sleep on," he said. He pointed to rivets in the ends of the shelving units. "See here. This is where the...chains would have been secured to keep the...the slaves from moving around too much."

At that, Catheryn's foot bumped something on the ground. Something heavy and metallic.

"Shackles..." she said. "Oh my God," she mumbled. "These were the bonds of slavery that held my ancestors." She held her hands to her mouth and did her best to stifle tears.

Rainier put his arm around her. "It's all right."

It wasn't all right. But he didn't know what else to say, and for whatever reason, Catheryn seemed comforted by his words anyway. She turned to him and wrapped her arms around him. He had no way of knowing what she was feeling or thinking. All he could do was be there for her.

"What...what is that?" she asked.

Rainier turned to see what she was looking at. Behind him, as the sun set and the rays hit the back of the hull, a symbol was appearing. Catheryn walked over to it to get a better look. As she ran her hands over it, the symbol became clearer.

"This...this is it," she said. "The symbol I drew. This is it! The symbol of the hoodoo witches who were on this ship. They must have painted it. Maybe it gave them hope, or power, or..."

Rainier nodded. "Amazing. And you drew it. It called to you throughout time and over such a distance." He truly was in awe of what was transpiring before him. Surely it was fate that brought him and Catheryn together.

"Come on!" she said, her tears giving way to excitement once again. "Who knows what else we will find!"

Rainier smiled as he followed Catheryn deeper into the ship.

Her happiness was infectious. He wished he could take away her pain and make her happy for the rest of her life.

As Catheryn ran, her foot kicked something small, sending it rolling across the floor. It glinted in the fading sunlight. She kneeled down to pick it up.

"What is it?" Rainier asked, running to her side. "Don't touch it before you know what it is."

Catheryn pulled her hand back. "It's a coin," she said. "A gold coin with...the symbol! It's the hoodoo symbol again!"

She picked it up and cradled it in both of her hands like something precious. "What does it mean?" she asked. "Do you think..."

Her eyes rolled back in her head, and her legs gave way out from under her. Rainier grabbed her before she fell to the deck. By now, he knew the signs. She was having a vision.

CHAPTER 13

Catheryn opened her eyes and found herself deep in the African jungle. Even though she had never been to Africa and really knew very little about it, somehow she instinctively knew where she was. She heard the sound of drums beating, the pounding so heavy it reverberated deep in her chest. She was walking toward the sound, and the light—the light of large fire that seemed to be drawing her toward it.

As she walked, she realized she was not alone. There were other people around her, people who were dancing, swaying, and waving their arms to the beat of the drums. They all had smiles on their faces. They were singing along with the music. They beckoned her to join them, gently reaching for her hands and her arms and pulling her toward the fire, the center of the festivities.

Catheryn felt safe. This place, these people, it all seemed so familiar. Like home. As she started to move with the music, along with the other people, the movements came naturally, as though she had grown up here.

She surprised herself when she started singing along with them. She had never heard the language before, but she knew it. They were praying for rain, for a good harvest, and for protection from the white ghosts that had been seen in the jungles near their village and had been wreaking havoc for other tribes.

An old woman, so old she was nearly completely hunched over and walked with a cane, walked up the fire and waved her hands over it. On her forehead was painted the symbol, the symbol Catheryn had drawn on her amulet, the symbol of the hoodoo witches. The old woman tossed some fragrant herbs into the fire. She looked through the flames, directly at Catheryn, and said, "Daughter of mine, do not fear. Your time will come."

The crack of a rifle rent the air, and everyone ran away screaming.

Catheryn got down on her knees and hid her face in her hands.

She was drenched.

She looked up and saw water pouring into the lower deck of the ship. There were hundreds of people crammed into the slave quarters as the ship sailed to the New World. There was a storm, and crashes of lightening were the only light in this damp, dark place. She stood, but as the ship heaved on the waves, she had to hold on to the stack of shelving to keep from falling over.

There was a large group of people huddled to one side of the room. Catheryn slowly made her way over to them. They parted as she approached. They were all watching a woman, a different woman, younger than the one who had spoken to her before, as she painted a symbol on the hull of the ship. The people had mixed their own blood with ash and water to make the paint she was using. They were all chanting as the woman painted. They were patting their hands on the floor to make a drumming noise.

Save us, protect us

Release us, find freedom

Catheryn could once again understand the words they were saying. The woman finished her painting and got down on her knees and started drumming and chanting along with the others.

The symbol was the one Catheryn had seen on the wrecked ship. The symbol of the hoodoo witches.

The ship lurched forward as it came to a sudden stop. All of the people were thrown forward as several of the boards to the front hull snapped, letting sand and water into the ship. Catheryn grabbed onto a crate and held on for dear life.

When Catheryn opened her eyes, she was lying on the beach, the sun warming her skin. She looked around and saw that a large group of people had gathered around some small boats. It looked as though they were saying goodbye.

She walked over to join them and saw that they were taking many provisions with them. They weren't planning on coming back. One of them was carrying the book she found in the village, the book about hoodoo magic.

After the ship had crashed on the shore, the people escaped the slavers and built a new life for themselves on the island. But they had grown too prosperous. They island could no longer sustain them. So they decided to disperse, travel to other islands, form new colonies, take their traditional practices with them.

A young woman who had been settling her children in one of the boats walked over to Catheryn. She was wearing a silver pendant on a leather cord around her neck. The symbol of the hoodoo witches.

"Do not fear, my daughter," the woman said as she took Catheryn's face in her hands. "We will meet again."

Catheryn felt her eyes well with tears. "Don't leave me," she cried. "Please don't go…"

Catheryn rubbed her eyes, and when she opened them again, she was in a slum in NOLA. She knew it because she had been there before. She grew up there. In a tiny one-room shack, two little girls were attending their ailing parents.

The older of the two girls was Catheryn. The other girl was her sister, Eva.

The older girl wetted a cloth and rubbed it over her mother's forehead. She had a fever, but shuddered as if chilled. She had a rash all over her body. Typhoid.

Catheryn kneeled down and put her arms around the two girls to comfort them. Her mother reached out and gripped her hand. Catheryn saw the hoodoo symbol had been tattooed on her wrist.

"We will always be with you," her mother said. "I am watching you. Do not fear, my daughter."

"Mommy!" Catheryn exclaimed. "Mommy, don't leave me!"

Catheryn held the younger version of herself and her little sister in her arms as they all wept together.

When Catheryn opened her eyes again, she was still weeping, but Rainier was holding her. She was back inside the wrecked ship. She held onto Rainier as sobs wracked her body. He didn't say anything, he just held her, rocking her gently.

Finally, she calmed down enough to tell him what happened.

"I am a full-blood hoodoo witch," she said. She was still holding the coin in her hand. She gripped it tightly and held it to her chest. Then she placed it safely in the amulet bag round her neck. "My family was part of a powerful hoodoo tribe in Africa. Because the slavers had guns, they were able to capture my ancestors and force them onto a slave ship. *This* slave ship.

"But they escaped. They drew this symbol on the wall..." She stood up and ran to the symbol, running her fingers over it. It was as though she could feel the heartbeats of every person whose blood was used to paint the symbol. "When they painted the symbol, the ship crashed, and they were freed.

"They lived here on the island, but eventually they set out for other islands so they could spread hoodoo magic to the New World. They founded that other village you ransacked. That's why it was protected from pirates for so long."

"But why did the protection fail?" Rainier asked. "Why were we able to find that village now?"

"The pure-blood witches eventually died out," she said. "Maybe the protections the witches had placed over the village eventually faded away."

"Or maybe they faltered because you were meant to find that book," Rainier said.

Catheryn shrugged. "Maybe. But somehow, my parents found their way to NOLA. They were the last pure-blood hoodoo witch couple. They died of typhoid fever. I guess their bloodline passed to me."

"So, you are the last pure-blood hoodoo witch?" Rainier asked.

"It's possible," Catheryn said. "But I had...*have* a sister. Eva."

"The one you sold yourself into slavery to protect," Rainier said.

"Yes," Catheryn confirmed. "That means there's at least two of us. I don't remember her having any hoodoo powers, but if mine manifested late, maybe hers did, too. I have to find her."

"So the Hoodoo Queen of NOLA," Rainier said, "she's not a full-blood hoodoo witch like you?"

"I don't think so," Catheryn said. "She is a very powerful witch, but she is not full-blooded."

"I had a vision, too," he said. "I didn't want tell you because I didn't want to upset you. But I saw her rounding up all the humans. I think she is going to do something to them."

"What?" Catheryn asked, her eyebrows tight.

"I'm not sure," he said. "My vision was short, fleeting, after one of the times I fed from you. But I'm certain the humans are in danger. We could go back to NOLA. You could defeat her."

Catheryn snorted. "Defeat her? Me? Are you daft? I can't defeat the Hoodoo Queen."

"But your powers have been growing by the day. By the time we get back to NOLA, your powers could be fully formed."

"Or they might not be," she said. "Or even if they were, I can't control them."

"You could train them," he said. "Just like any fighting skill."

Catheryn shook her head. "Why do you care so much?" she asked. "You don't care about humans."

"I cared about you when I thought you were one," he said.

"Only because you needed a dinner," she said. "Are you worried the queen is going to control your only source of food?"

"That's not it," he said. "I thought...I thought you would want to protect them. I was offering to help you."

"And protect yourself," Catheryn said. "Your way of life. You only want to defeat the Hoodoo Queen so you can control NOLA yourself."

"The thought never even crossed my mind," he said. "How can you think so little of me?"

"I can't even escape from you!" Catheryn said. "How do you think I could possibly fight and win against the Hoodoo Queen?"

Rainier paused. "You...you want to escape from me?" he asked as though hurt.

"I'm your slave!" she said pointedly. "I'm not here of my own free will."

"But you agreed to be my devotee," he said.

"I didn't have a choice," she said. "If you weren't feeding from me it would just be someone else you'd feed from. I was protecting the villagers."

"I brought you here," he said, motioning toward the ship. "I'm helping you find out who you are. Helping you find your powers, making you stronger. What else do I have to do to get you to trust me?"

"Set me free," she said. "Grant me my freedom. Let me return to NOLA and find my sister."

Rainier didn't say anything.

Catheryn nodded. "That's what I thought."

"We better get back to the ship," Rainier said in a defeated voice. They walked in silence back through the jungle along the path he had created for them earlier. They got in the lifeboat and rowed back to the ship.

When they arrived back at the ship, the crew had all returned. They looked exhausted and angry. Catheryn didn't care about them, though. She simply returned to her...to *Rainier's* quarters. She went to the desk and went back to reading her hoodoo book. She could feel the ship pull up anchor and gently rock as it made its way back out to sea.

A little while later, Rainier returned to the room. He looked sad and defeated, but Catheryn did not even greet him.

"The crew is angry," he said. "They didn't find the treasure, obviously. They feel like I deliberately misled them."

"And they are right," Catheryn said.

Rainier nodded. "I guess I'm not as clever as I thought," he conceded. "They are curious why I would bring them here, send them on a wild goose chase, and then disappear into the forest with my...slave."

Catheryn looked at him and raised an eyebrow.

"They are grumbling against me," he said.

Catheryn shrugged and went back to her book. "Not my problem."

"Oh, yes it is," he said. "You are my personal slave. The men have their eye on you. Without me to enforce the rations, how long do you think those poor souls below deck will last? How long do you think *you* will last?"

"Are you threatening me?" she asked, slowly standing.

"No," he said. "I'm warning you. If you don't learn to defend yourself, and something happens to me, you're dead."

CHAPTER 14

Rainier stood across from Catheryn, each with a staff in hand. It was the next morning, and Rainier had pushed all the furniture in the room against the walls and locked the door. The room was now large and open enough that Rainier could give Catheryn a basic sword-fighting lesson.

Catheryn looked disinterested, letting her staff dangle at her side. "This is stupid," she said. "Why are we doing this? I'll never learn enough to make a difference."

"If you can't control your magical powers," Rainier explained, "you should learn to defend yourself the old-fashioned way. Who knows, maybe a good ol' training session will teach you something about hard work and discipline and will help you train your hoodoo powers as well."

"So I can help you take down the Hoodoo Queen?" Catheryn asked.

"You have no love for the woman," he said. "Is my plan so terrible? Wouldn't NOLA be better off without her?"

"It depends on who takes her place," Catheryn said.

"Well, if you don't think it should be me," Rainier said as he raised his staff and started circling Catheryn, "maybe it should be you."

Catheryn laughed.

Rainier tapped her stick with his own, getting her to raise it. "What's so funny?"

"I was born in a slum, grew up a slave, and now live as a bloodbag for a vampire. How exactly am I supposed to defeat the most powerful witch in NOLA and become a queen myself?"

"Well, you'll never accomplish anything with that attitude," he said. "Now raise your sword."

"It's a stick," she said, but raised it anyway.

"It is the only thing standing between you and certain death," he said as he assumed a fighting stance. Catheryn mimicked him. Rainier moved to her side and helped correct her posture. "Curve your back like this," he said, placing his hand along her spine. "And turn your hips like this." He stood back and admired his work. "Beautiful."

"Better hurry up," she said. "This *sword* is heavy."

"You will have to build up your strength. Now, swing right, then return to this position. No, remember your back. Again."

It took a few tries, but soon, Catheryn was able to swing her sword and return to the correct first position with ease.

"Excellent," Rainier said. "Now, try to advance. Take a step forward, but retain the original position. Very good."

After only training for a few minutes, Rainier realized that Catheryn was actually a very apt student, when she put her mind to it.

"I think we are ready for you start taking on your first opponent," he said, stepping forward and raising his stick.

"Go easy on me," she said.

"Never," he replied.

He advanced toward her and swung, but she easily deflected his blow.

"Excellent!" he said, genuinely pleased.

Catheryn smiled, though the flush in her cheeks made him think she was actually embarrassed by his praise. She was likely also still upset with what had happened the previous night. Why didn't he release her? He shook his head to clear his mind. When it came to swordplay, he needed to concentrate on the task at hand.

Catheryn was moving quite well, and gaining in her confidence. Before long, she was taking risks and advancing on him of her own accord. She was keeping him on his toes. He would have to show her what a master swordsman could do.

She advanced, slashing to the right and left. He feinted a retreat, but he quickly came up by her side and used his sword against hers to spin her around. To her surprise, she ended up wrapped in his arms and laughed.

"How did this happen?" she asked, looking up at him with a smile.

"I couldn't let you get too cocky," he said.

A silence passed between them. It felt good, holding her in his arms, and she didn't seem to be in a hurry to remove herself, but there was an awkwardness as well. She was still hurt and angry that she was his slave, and he was hurt that she didn't trust him. But neither of those issues could be resolved right now, so Rainier finally released her.

"You are improving quickly," he said. "I think we are ready to move you to real blades."

"Are you joking?" she asked.

"No," he said as he went to a trunk and pulled out a slim rapier for her. "It is highly unusual, I admit, but your progress has been amazing. Almost preternatural."

She blushed at that. She still lacked confidence in her abilities and doubted the truth of her own visions. But Rainier knew she was special. He could see it in the remarkable progress she had made day by day. He decided to make it his personal mission to help her confidence grow until she saw the same strong, powerful, beautiful woman he did.

But what would he do with her then? If she truly came into her powers and knew her own strength, she could certainly leave him. Would she kill him in the process? The man who had kidnapped her, drank her blood, and killed her fellow slaves? He certainly hoped not. He hoped she would see him for the good he had done for her. After all, she never would have discovered who she was or even found the book or the ship if they had never met.

He had to help her see that their shared enemy was the Hoodoo Queen, not each other.

"Why is my blade so small compared to yours?" she asked.

"Every person has a blade that is right for him," he said.

Catheryn cocked her eyebrow.

"Or her," he amended. "When a sword is used correctly, a small thin blade can do just as much damage as a large one. It is more important to have a blade that fits your body type and fighting style than to have the biggest one in the fight."

"Do you think that is true in all fights?" she asked. "A person smaller and weaker can take down someone bigger and stronger with the right skills."

"Certainly," he said. "I have small crewmen and large crewmen. I even have female crewmen, though I would dare you to pick them out." Catheryn's eyes widened at that, and Rainier laughed as she obviously began trying to figure out which of the ship's crew were women. "The point is, they can all hold their own in a battle. I depend on each one of them. But they all know their own abilities."

Catheryn nodded, but said nothing.

"You are beginning to believe in yourself, aren't you?" Rainier asked. "You are wondering if even though you are younger and your abilities not yet fully formed, if you could take on the Hoodoo Queen, if you were trained properly."

"It's a fool's errand," she said as she raised her sword. "Let's just focus on this."

Rainier nodded as he took his position. "Advance."

~

By the time the sun was setting, Catheryn had improved by leaps and bounds. She had achieved a level of sword mastery that would take years for a normal human. She was in awe of her own progress.

"If I wasn't experiencing this for myself, I'd never believe it," she said as she leaned against the desk, panting.

"Think about what you could accomplish if you applied the same training techniques to your magic," Rainier said.

"Maybe," Catheryn said softly.

Rainier could sense she was starting to believe in herself, but she was also scared. Her whole world had changed in the last few days. It was a lot to take in.

"Why don't I go see the cook and have dinner brought up," Rainier said, sheathing his sword in the scabbard at his belt. "Maybe I can even find a good bottle of port to celebrate with."

"You still drink alcohol?" she asked. "And eat food?"

"Of course," he said. "Why do you think I have a cook?"

"I thought he just cooked for the human chattel," she said.

"No, we all eat food," he said. "Just some of us more than others. Anyway, I'll be back soon."

When Rainier got up on the main deck, it was eerily quiet. Usually the evenings were a time of relaxation and revelry for the crew. There would be people singing, playing music, dancing, playing games of chance. But tonight, there was no reveling. The deck was surprisingly empty, and the few men who were milling about were not in a celebratory mood.

Rainier went up to the helm. Mathis was there, minding the wheel.

"How goes it?" Rainier asked.

"Calm," Mathis said. "Too calm."

"It is quiet," Rainier said. "There is a...tension in the air, wouldn't you say?"

"Aye, that I would." Mathis didn't look at Rainier, but kept his eyes straight ahead as he steered.

"As my first mate," Rainier said, "I hope you will be honest with me."

"As you've been honest with me, sir?" Mathis asked, clearly implying that Rainier had not been honest with him.

"This is my ship and my crew," Rainier said. "It goes where I bid it and does as I command."

"You and I both know that ain't how this works," Mathis said. "These men rely on you to do what is best for them."

"And they think I'm not acting in their best interest?" Rainier asked.

"Sending them off on some fake treasure hunt while you gallivant off in the forest with that...that weird girl?" Mathis asked. "Not bloody likely."

"It's not my fault the map didn't pan out," Rainier said. "There was always the chance it was a fake or a decoy or had already been plundered. That's a pirate's life, is it not?"

"If you had been by the men's side they might agree with you," Mathis said. "But you didn't go with them. And you didn't wait on the ship like you said. You at least lied to them on that score."

"Fine, one lie in all my years of captaining this ship," Rainier said. "Can they not grant me leniency for one screw up? Did it not occur to them that maybe my intention was to stay, but plans changed unexpectedly?"

"It's more than that, sir," Mathis said. "It's that girl. You ain't been quite right since we brought her on board."

"What do you mean?" Rainier asked. Of course it was true. He was feeling weaker and less vampirish since he started feeding from Catheryn, but he had tried to act the same around the crew.

"You're a terrible actor," Mathis said. "But that was what always made you a great captain. The men knew you to be sincere. Now? They know you ain't right. If they feel you could be leading them astray, they won't tolerate ya for long."

"What should I do?" Rainier asked. "How can I gain back their trust?"

"Get rid of the girl," Mathis said. "Leave her at the next settlement we come across. Or just put her in a lifeboat and shove her off. Get her off this ship."

"As you so eloquently put it, Mathis, not bloody likely," Rainier tried to say with a bit of lightness in his voice. But Mathis was having none of it.

"She's bad luck," Mathis said. "She may be human, but she's bewitched ya. The men can't trust your decisions as long as she's on board."

"You are talking complete and utter nonsense," Rainier said. "Do my men really think me so weak that I would be influenced by some woman?"

Mathis shook his head. "I'm your mate and your friend. If you won't listen to me, what does that tell you?"

"Mind how she goes," Rainier said, giving Mathis the order to focus on the ship, and stomped away.

"Aye, sir," Mathis called out after him.

Rainier couldn't believe what he was hearing. After all these years, after all he'd done for his crew, they would doubt his ability to lead them just because he kept a strange woman in his room. He'd known pirate captains with much worse habits than that. There was Captain Rosenthal, who not only drank blood, but tortured his human captives, often flaying them alive right on the deck. There was Captain Blackheart—he gave himself that name —who would not just make men walk the plank, but would shoot them out of a cannon for insubordination. Then there was Captain Lacroix, as dangerous as she was beautiful, who took a whip to her lovers, as Rainier well knew.

Rainier made his way to the cook's station and ordered a meal of roasted chicken and vegetables be plated. He then visited the wine room to find an appropriate pairing.

As much as he wanted to keep Catheryn with him, though, shouldn't the needs of his crew come first? If the crew wanted him to throw her overboard, shouldn't he do it as a show of good faith even if it was an extreme request?

But he was the captain. If his crew was grumbling, he should be more stern with them. Keep them in line. Keep them to their work.

He picked a stout port and took the bottle back to the cook's station. He took the tray of food and the bottle of port back up to the deck.

Keeping Catheryn on board was good for the crew anyway, even if they didn't know it. She was growing in power. He needed her on their side. He was certain he could use her against the Hoodoo Queen eventually if he kept working on her.

But what if she didn't? Even though she knew her powers were growing, she still seemed averse to the idea of going up against the queen. Would he be able to justify keeping her on board if she refused to take the queen down?

Rainier walked slowly as the realization dawned on him. He didn't want her to go. No matter what, he wanted to keep her with him on the ship. He didn't want to set her free because he didn't want her to leave. He was feeling something growing between them. He thought about how she saved his life on the beach, and how he held her when she cried after she saw the vision of her ancestors. He wanted to have her in his life and be a part of hers. He wanted to be there with her through the good times and the bad. They made a good team. They could be excellent partners.

He was falling in love with her.

CHAPTER 15

Catheryn paced Rainier's quarters. She was warm and sweaty from their training session, and her heart was still racing. She felt anxious and jittery. She practiced a few moves with her sword on her own. She looked at her stance in a full-length mirror that was sitting in one corner of the room. She barely recognized herself.

She was standing tall, not cowering with her chin to her chest. Brandishing her sword with a smile on her face, she felt strong, powerful. She had never felt this way before.

She had Rainier to thank for unlocking this side of her. He believed in her, and he was forcing her to find the power hidden deep inside.

Rainier. The pirate. The vampire.

The murderer.

The smile ran away from her face, and she turned away from her reflection, ashamed of herself. How could she think so kindly of him? He was her owner, her master, nothing more. She was only food to him. He only kidnapped her because she had a pretty face and a warm pulse. She didn't mean more to him that the dozens of other slaves he could have chosen.

At least, that's why she was initially brought to the ship. But things had changed. He knew she was not a suitable food source for him, but he kept her on board. He was even trying to help her find out who—what—she was. He volunteered to take her to the shipwreck. He offered to teach her sword fighting. She hadn't asked him for anything.

Except to release her.

When she asked him to set her free, he refused. He couldn't grant her this one request. Of course, if he had released her, she probably would have jumped into the sea and swam away. She wouldn't have cared if the giant spider was still alive or if she would starve to death, she would have left. The idea of being Rainier's kept slave, as his possible food source, still soured her stomach. She couldn't really blame him for refusing to release her, could she? Not when they both knew she would run.

Or would she have?

She remembered reading in the hoodoo book that a pure hoodoo witch's powers were innate. Of course, training can help the powers become stronger more quickly, but even without aid, the powers would eventually manifest themselves. And she had seen this happening. Even before Rainier and his men attacked the Hoodoo House, she had seen small instances of her powers awaking. She shuddered as she thought about the witch she had injured in the kitchen and left locked in a closet.

And her powers had grown by leaps and bounds since her arrival on the ship. Rainier had noticed that her powers seemed to come to life when she was in danger, and she had experienced more than her fair share of life-threatening moments since she came aboard. If she had never been brought to the ship, her powers certainly wouldn't have grown so quickly.

Would she have left?

If her hoodoo powers were innate and growing, why didn't she use them to escape? If he wouldn't set her free, it was up to her to free herself. So why didn't she? She never wanted to be here. Even now, after all they had been through, it wasn't her choice to stay. Rainier was holding her captive. No matter how kind to her he was, no matter how much he helped her powers improve, she was his slave and was being forced to do his bidding. The fact that she was his slave should trump everything else. It should render all the good he had done irrelevant. Logically, she knew this.

So why was she staying?

She couldn't deny that something was growing between them. She had agreed to be his "devotee" only to keep him from feeding on someone else. But she had to admit that the last time he fed from her, she wanted him to bite her…wanted him to do so much more to her. She remembered his kisses on her neck and his hands on her thighs. And on the beach, after she saved his life. She was surprised he didn't throw her down on the sand and take her. She wouldn't have stopped him.

Was she crazy? Was she staying, risking her life, submitting to the will of a dangerous vampire and pirate because she wanted to sleep with him?

Or was it something more?

Just thinking about Rainier in that way made her feel hot again. The thought of leaving him filled her with a different kind of anxiety. The thought of leaving him behind, never seeing him again, made her…sad. She must surely be losing her mind if she was developing feelings for a vampire.

She couldn't admit to these growing feelings…not yet.

As she paced, she caught a glimpse of herself in the mirror again. But she looked…different. She took a step closer to get a better look. As she did, the mirror seemed to pulse, then a dark inkiness began to fill the glass, like the feathers of a crow spreading out. Her face changed and morphed into the Hoodoo Queen.

"My child," the face spoke.

Catheryn gasped and took a step back. Was she dreaming? Having another vision?

"No," the Hoodoo Queen said, as if able to read Catheryn's thoughts. "I am reaching out to you across the ocean. You have traveled far, my little one."

"I am not your anything," Catheryn spat. "At one time I was your slave, but not now. You gave me away. I belong here now."

"You belong with your people," the queen said. Catheryn's heart skipped a beat. She suddenly felt afraid, but she didn't say anything. If the Hoodoo Queen could speak to her across the ocean, read her thoughts, what else could she do?

"You had to know I would find out, Catheryn," the queen said. "I found Nathalie in the closet. She was as angry as a hornet, but she couldn't deny what she saw. And I can't deny what I have seen, what you have learned. You are not the human we all thought, are you? You are of pure hoodoo blood. With the right training, you could be the most powerful witch in the NOLA Division."

"And where would that leave you?" Catheryn asked, incensed. Everyone wanted to use her for something. Both Rainier—the powerful vampire—and the Hoodoo Queen—the powerful witch—only wanted her to help them achieve their own ends.

"I would be at you side," the queen said sweetly, motherly. "As your mentor and the person with experience ruling over a Division, you and I could be an unstoppable team. Together, we could vanquish the vampires and bring peace and security to NOLA. Then, who knows? With your powers, we could look for a way to connect with the other Divisions. A way to save the world."

Catheryn felt a wave of emotion wash over her. Even though slaves were not included in talks about the current state of the world, they all knew things were slowly getting worse. The tides were rising and food was being rationed more strictly. She didn't know why this was happening or if it was something that could be fixed without connecting to the other Divisions, but if there was a chance she could use her powers to help make the world, or just their little corner of it, better, she had to try.

But could she trust the queen? Could she trust Rainier? She was at a loss.

"Your magic," the queen continued, "it called out to me. I felt it. When you picked up that coin, when your mind was opened, it sent a vibration across the whole world. I felt it. It called to me. It told me to find you.

"I know I did wrong by you," she continued. "I had no idea who you were, and I treated you badly. I can admit when I do wrong. Let me help you. Let me make amends. Come home, Catheryn."

Catheryn knew the queen was trying to sweet-talk her, but she chuffed at the reference to "home." She had been a slave in that house. She had no parents, no siblings. The other slaves, the humans, had looked out for her and treated her more lovingly than the witches had. Then she remembered what Rainier had told her about his vision.

"The humans," Catheryn said. "What is your plan for them? You said we would vanquish the vampires, but what about the humans?"

The queen paused, which surprised Catheryn. She decided to push her advantage.

"I'll know if you lie to me," she said. She had no way of knowing if this was true, but she hoped the queen wouldn't know either. She couldn't know just how powerful Catheryn was or would become.

"The humans will have their place in society," the queen said. "We cannot live without them the way we can without blood-sucking vampires."

"In your home they are slaves," Catheryn said. "Is that an example of the place they will have in your 'harmonious' society?"

The queen shook her head. "Catheryn, child, come home. The humans will have their place. We can work out the details when you are here, when we rule together. You can help me decide what to do with them."

While she wanted the chance to help the other humans, a little warning bell was going off in the back of her head. She had lived in the home of the hoodoo queen for too long to believe she would do right by people she thought beneath her. Catheryn's heart started to race again. She couldn't go back. Not yet. Or at least not on the queen's terms.

"I'm sorry," Catheryn said, though she wasn't sorry at all. "I don't think I can accept your offer."

"Catheryn," the queen said sternly, the mirror growing darker and deeper, like a black hole, "you will come back. One way or another. You can come home as my guest, as my protégé, under my protection...or you can come back in chains."

Catheryn felt her heart beat hard in her chest as a pulse boomed out of her body, shattering the mirror. The queen was gone, for now. The thought of once again being in chains terrified her. She couldn't do it. She couldn't be a slave again. She might be a slave to Rainier, but he didn't lock her up. If she had to choose between Rainier and the Hoodoo Queen, Rainier would be her choice.

She wasn't sure what Rainier could do, or what they could do together, but she needed to tell him about the queen. They would have to work together. She threw open the door to the cabin, her small rapier still in hand, and ran out on to the deck to find him.

"Rainier?" she called out.

It was dark, and she got turned around. She couldn't remember the way to the cook's station.

It was quiet out, but she noticed that there were lots of pirates on the deck. She suddenly realized that she was surrounded. They were slowly advancing toward her, hemming her in. She looked from one side to the other, but there was nowhere to go. She started to raise her hands, hoping her powers would come to her defense, but then she felt a hand grip her wrist tightly.

She turned and locked eyes with Mathis.

"Hello, deary," he said menacingly. "A little bird is looking for you."

He laughed as he pointed to the black crow sitting upon his shoulder. The crew moved in even tighter and laughed as the crow cawed.

CHAPTER 16

R ainier dropped the tray of food and drink when he saw Catheryn surrounded by the crew.

"What is going on?" he demanded. "Back to your quarters, all of you!"

Mathis stepped forward with an air of surety, a strange black crow sitting on his shoulder. Rainier wondered for a moment where he had seen a crow recently, then he remembered that the Hoodoo Queen had a crow when he faced her at the Hoodoo House.

"What is the meaning of this?" Rainier asked.

"I gave you a choice, cap'n," Mathis said. "I tried to warn ya. It seemed simple enough to me: the crew or the woman. You chose poorly."

Some of the men laughed while others grumbled angrily.

"*I* am the captain," Rainier said. "*I* give the orders. I don't take ultimatums."

"You ain't the captain no more," Mathis said, snatching the hat off Rainier's head. "The Hoodoo Queen made me a generous offer. She wants the girl. In exchange, she'll reward the entire crew with gold. As a bonus, she said she'd take you off our hands as well." Mathis arranged the tricorn hat on his head, adjusting it just so. He ran his fingers over his eyebrows and then straightened his vest. "I'm the captain now. You and the missy will be taken to the brig while we make for NOLA, where we will hand you over to the queen."

"You think you can trust her?" Catheryn asked. "You think the Hoodoo Queen will actually honor her word to a bunch of vampires?"

"Stay out of this, Catheryn," Rainier growled, never averting his glare from Mathis. "But she asks a good question. You think that woman will really let you sail away from NOLA with your ship, your gold, and your heads in tact?"

"We have what she wants," Mathis said. "We also outnumber her. She's a smart business woman. She'll do as she says."

"There's just one problem," Rainier said, drawing his blade. "I'll not go quietly."

The men all drew their swords, but Mathis held up his hand. "No, no, lads. I'll take care of this. If I can't defeat him, I'll not be worthy of being called captain."

He drew his own sword as the others took a step back.

Catheryn held her sword tightly and held up her other hand, as if she might try to summon her magic.

"No," Rainier told her again. "This is a pirate matter. A matter of honor. You stay out of it."

Catheryn looked hurt, but she took a step back.

Rainier turned back to Mathis and raised his sword. The crow flew from Mathis's shoulder and up to one of the rafters for a prime viewing spot. The captain and his first mate circled each other for a moment, each sizing up the other.

Under normal circumstances, Mathis wouldn't stand a chance against Rainier, and they both knew that. Rainier had proven time and again over the years that he was the strongest vampire on the ship, and one of the strongest of all the vampire pirate captains. Yet since he had been feeding on Catheryn, his power had been waning. Mathis knew that Rainier hadn't been himself lately, but surely he had no way of knowing just how weak Rainier had become...unless the Hoodoo Queen told him that as well.

How did the queen even know where they were? How did she know where to send the raven? Was she in communication with Catheryn? Did they have some sort of witch connection? He would have to confront her about that after this was over. *If* he survived. He had to. Both of their lives depended on it.

Mathis charged, surprising Rainier. Mathis showed no fear, no hesitation as he used a foreswing, followed by a quick backswing. Rainier dodged the first, but caught his bearings and met the second with his cutlass. Mathis continued to advance, and Rainier stepped back, back, back.

Mathis look a large step forward and sliced uncomfortably close to Rainier's chest. Mathis's blade made a clean cut through Rainier's shirt, barely missing the flesh.

Rainier felt his anger rise. The little blood he had in his body boiled and surged through him. He blocked Mathis's next blow and pushed back against the attack, sending Mathis reeling backward. Rainier swung again, but this time he missed. Mathis smirked, unconcerned about Rainier's sudden surge of energy.

The two men continued advancing, retreating, advancing on one another, each getting the upper hand in their turn. But Rainier could feel his strength growing. He had more to lose...too much. He felt a rage burning within him. He tossed the rules of swordsmanship over the railing and grabbed Mathis's arm before punching him in the face. He heard the groan of the crowd, but that only made him angrier. They would all be next. Faithless traitors!

Mathis looked up at Rainier as blood streamed from his nose. He tried to regain his composure and his standing, but Rainier bent his arm back, forcing him to drop his sword. Mathis fell to his knees.

During the course of the battle, a storm had started to move in.

The ship swayed from side to side in the salty breeze. A few raindrops pattered on the deck as thunder rumbled in the distance.

"You're not the vampire I was once so proud to serve," Mathis groaned.

"No, I'm not," Rainier replied.

With that, he released Mathis's arm. He gripped his sword with both hands and sliced through Mathis's neck like it was paper. For a second, the whole ship went silent. Then Mathis's head fell from his body with a sickening thunk.

Rainier kicked the body over the side of the ship but picked up the head by its hair and showed it to the crew.

"Who's next?" he asked.

The move did not have the effect he had hoped. He thought the crew would be cowed back into submission. Instead, it seemed to have angered them further. They all once again drew their swords and took a step toward him.

"That weren't honorable!" one of the men yelled.

"You're no pirate!" another said.

"We'll not follow you," another said, followed by a round of jeers.

"Come on," another yelled. "Look, he's winded from battle! He can't take us all on. We'll kill him and take the girl to the witch queen ourselves. We'll still get our reward, and then we'll choose our own captain!"

The crew hollered their agreement as they continued to advance on Rainier. He tossed Mathis's head over the side of the ship and held his sword up. His eyes scanned the deck for Catheryn, but he didn't see her. Maybe she slipped away during the fight.

At least one of them might survive this night.

CHAPTER 17

Rainier had told Catheryn to stay out of his fight with Mathis, so she hung back, away from the crowd. The fight was intense, so after a moment, it seemed as if everyone had forgotten Catheryn was there.

She moved further away from the crowd until she was against the railing on the other side. She looked out, and all she could see was open sea. If she could just get a glimpse of land, she would be brave enough to try to swim away. But out here, she had no idea which way to go and would surely drown before she got very far. More than that, a storm was brewing. The wind had picked up and drops of rain were starting to fall. The ship was gently rocking as the sky darkened.

Her only hope was for Rainier to win the battle and get his crew and ship back. She looked at the battle just as Rainier sliced through Mathis's neck. She put her hand to her mouth to stifle her gasp as Mathis's head slipped from his body. Then she watched as the crew began to advance on Rainier. One of them shouted something about still returning to the Hoodoo Queen. Even Rainier looked nervous.

As two of the pirates moved in on Rainier, she could see that he was weak. He had mentioned to her that since he had been feeding on her, he had felt weaker, but the fight with Mathis must have sapped a lot of his strength. As he struggled to defend himself, Catheryn felt a rumbling inside her, deep in the pit of her stomach. Pirate business or no, Rainier needed her help.

The book had said that her hoodoo powers should be innate. And she could feel the power coursing through her, as though an energy long asleep within her had awakened. As the ship began to rock more violently in the growing storm, Catheryn raised her arms, and a wave crashed over the deck, knocking many of the pirates off their feet and drenching them.

Everyone looked in the direction the wave had come from and saw Catheryn, standing tall and proud, a look of determination on her face. Lightning cracked behind her as the storm grew.

"Stop the witch!" someone yelled.

The whole crew jumped to action, scrambling to their feet on the wet deck to move toward her. Rainier ran down the deck toward the lifeboats.

Catheryn caused another wave to crash over the deck. This time, some of the crew were washed overboard.

"She means to sink us!" someone yelled.

"Stop her!" another screamed. Up above them, the crow cawed anxiously.

"Catheryn!" Rainier yelled. Catheryn looked to him and saw he was in the lifeboat, waving her over.

Catheryn seemed to call upon the wind itself, which pushed the crewmen back, not allowing them to advance toward her. She ran toward Rainier and jumped into the lifeboat. Rainier worked the pulley to lower the craft into the water, but it was going much too slowly. The crew had managed to make their way to the side of the ship and were looking down at Rainier and Catheryn. The pirates worked against Rainier to raise the boat back up.

After a moment of struggling, Rainier had had enough. He used his sword to cut the ropes and free the boat. Catheryn looked over the side and saw that they were still more than halfway up the ship.

"Are you crazy?" she screamed through the howling wind. "The boat will shatter!"

"We don't have a choice!" he yelled back. "Hold on!"

Stupid man! Catheryn thought to herself. She hooked her leg around one of the seats, but raised her arms once again. As Rainier cut the last rope and they started to fall, a strong gust of wind came up from below, slowing their descent. They still hit the water hard, but not hard enough to damage the integrity of their little escape vessel.

Rainier nodded his thanks to Catheryn. Then he pulled out the oars and started to row them away from the ship.

The pirates were not through yet, though. *The Cursed Storm* slowly began to turn toward them, and the men were readying the cannons.

Rainier's face dropped. It appeared to Catheryn that he hadn't really considered just how foolish his heroic plan was. They could not outrun a ship like *The Cursed Storm*. The ship would either run them down, crushing their lifeboat, or the crew would blow them out of the water with a cannon ball. Rainier had no way to fight back or defend them. In his current weakened state, he did not have the strength to row them away quickly enough.

Catheryn stood in the lifeboat and turned to face *The Cursed Storm*. She would revel in the fact she was saving Rainier's life twice in a matter of minutes later.

For the first time, she had no trouble calling forth and controlling her powers. The ocean seemed to be at her command. She waved her arms back and forth, churning the sea. Out of a small vortex in the water, a mighty stream of water sprouted forth and stabbed into the side of the ship, creating a huge hole.

The pirates on board ran about in a panic as the ship started taking on water and lilting to the side. Instantly, Catheryn and

Rainier were forgotten as the pirates focused on keeping their ship from sinking.

Catheryn turned back to Rainier and sat down, saying nothing, though she assumed the smirk on her face said more than enough. Rainier was not smiling, but was focused on rowing their little boat as far away from *The Cursed Storm* as possible.

The rain was still falling, in larger and more frequent drops now, and the wind was still blowing. Catheryn's sense of satisfaction waned as she watched the billowing clouds grow darker and larger. There was still no land in sight. They would not be able to escape the storm.

"Why didn't you tell me about the queen?" Rainier finally asked. "How long has she been in contact with you?"

"While you were gone getting us food was the first time she contacted me," Catheryn said. "I had gone on deck to find you and tell you."

"What did she say?" he asked.

Catheryn shrugged. "She wanted me to come back. She somehow found out about my powers and wanted me to return so we could rule NOLA together."

Rainier looked pained at the words and shook his head. "So that was your plan? To go back?"

"How can you think that of me?" Catheryn said. "Do you think I'm stupid enough to trust the Hoodoo Queen? After all I suffered in her house? After all I have learned about my history? Myself?" She shook her head, disgusted.

"So what was your plan?" Rainier asked.

"I didn't have one," Catheryn said. "I was trying to find you so we could figure out what to do together."

Rainier nodded, sufficiently chastised. They were in this together, even more so now that they were trapped on this little boat in a growing storm.

"We won't get far in this little dingy," Catheryn said. "We should go back to the ship. Fight and take over *The Cursed Storm*."

"I'm not going back," Rainier said. "I've been deposed as captain. I can't go back."

"You're giving up?" Catheryn asked. "Just like that?"

"It…it's not a matter of giving up," Rainier said, annoyed. "It's a matter of honor. I lost the battle for my crew, for my ship. I can't go back. Besides, the ship is damaged. You and I wouldn't be able to repair it or steer it alone."

"But what about the other blood slaves?" Catheryn said. "The people who were kidnapped from the village? We can't just leave them. We could release them and they could help us."

Rainier shook his head. "They are probably already dead," Rainier said. "Do you remember what I told you before about me being the only thing keeping the crew from devouring the food rations?" Catheryn felt her face blanch as she slowly nodded. "I wasn't lying to you."

Catheryn felt sick to her stomach. All those poor people. She had completely forgotten about them in the heat of battle, and now they were most likely dead. Or they would be if the ship sank. Even if the pirates used the other lifeboats to escape, they probably wouldn't consider the humans they had below deck until it was too late. She needed to learn to keep her head when she was fighting. Keep every aspect of the situation in mind so she could make the best decisions.

"Catheryn," Rainier said, breaking into her thoughts. "Catheryn, you need to keep your wits about you. We have more pressing issues."

Catheryn looked at him, but he pointed behind her.

The storm had grown in ferocity, the clouds now black and churning nearly on top of them. The wind blew so hard Catheryn thought she would be blown away.

They were alone on the high sea in a tiny lifeboat with a storm barreling toward them and no land in sight.

CHAPTER 18

The lifeboat had a small sail, so Rainier did his best to hoist the rigging, hoping to catch the storm winds just right to blow them ahead of the storm.

The storm had started while he was on the deck. He had been a fool to jump into the lifeboat. They had a better chance of fighting off a hundred pirates than facing down a raging storm at sea in such a small boat.

Well, they had no choice but to face the storm now. Since Catheryn had disabled *The Cursed Storm*, they probably wouldn't fare much better on the ship even if they could make it back.

As Rainier squinted through the rain, even *The Cursed Storm* wasn't in his sights. He tightened the sail, and the little boat did pick up speed, skipping along the water in the storm's winds. Catheryn had her back to him, intently watching the storm with her long hair blowing in the breeze.

All of a sudden, she seemed in such control of her powers. On the deck of the ship, she just waved her arms and whatever she wanted to happen, happened. What gave her such a surge? Such control all of a sudden? Was it because of her contact with the Hoodoo Queen, or something else?

A crow cawed, and he looked up to see the Hoodoo Queen's pet flying overhead. It must have been trying to outfly the storm and get back home to its master. Maybe that meant he was sailing in the right direction—toward land. Any land.

The Hoodoo Queen was more powerful than he had given her credit for. He'd always known her power was not one to try and rival in NOLA itself, but he didn't think she could have any influence out *here*. How did she even contact Catheryn? Through that same bird? Was the Hoodoo Queen behind this storm? It seemed to billow up out of nowhere.

Rainier was getting paranoid. The world was no longer the way he thought. Everything was topsy-turvy. He needed to rest. He needed sustenance. He needed to recuperate. But first, they had to survive this storm. He needed to keep it together and summon the last of his strength. This storm would not defeat him. Not today.

"Catheryn!" he ordered. "Be sure to secure yourself to the boat. Use that rope there," he said, pointing to a rope that was tied to her seat. "Good. Now help me with this rigging!"

She came over to his side and held the ropes to the sail just so.

"Don't let go," he said. "And don't let her wobble. I need to be able to rely on which way the wind is going to blow the ship."

"Okay," she said as she tightly gripped the rope.

He leaned over the side of the boat to get a better look at the water beneath them. It was dark. The storm was a bad one. Even on a ship that was in prime form, they would be in for trouble.

Up ahead, rolling waves built toward them. He sat back by the oars and steered them toward the waves.

"What are you doing?" Catheryn screamed.

"We can't fight the sea, Catheryn," he said. "We have to roll with the waves or they'll bowl us over."

They both held their breath as they rode up and up the first wave. The boat softly descended on the other side.

Perfect, Rainier thought. But more were coming. He had to stay focused.

He positioned the boat to ride the next wave, and then the next. Between riding the waves and the wind blowing their sail, they were moving at a quick pace. Rainier started to think that they just might make it out of the storm when a monster wave— one that made his heart freeze in his chest—started cresting before them.

"Rainier..." Catheryn said softly. "We...we'll be able to ride that one like the others...right?"

Rainier couldn't lie to her, and he couldn't give her false hope.

Catheryn nodded and looked back at the wave. She stood and let go of the rigging.

"Catheryn!" Rainier called, gripping hold of the rope. As the sail flapped wildly, he yelled, "What are you doing? Have you gone mad?"

"Hold on," she said.

Rainier wanted to protest with every fiber of his being. This was not the way his years—decades—of pirating and steering a ship in a storm told him to act. But his pirating skills didn't matter here. He couldn't save them. If they had any hope, any chance, it would be in Catheryn's hands.

Catheryn faced the coming wave. She held her hands aloft, palms together, and then slowly separated them as the wave approached.

And just like that, the wave split apart.

Their little boat sailed right between the now two monster waves, and Rainier nearly laughed as he watched the water rise up around them.

"You did it!" he shouted over the rain as they cleared the wave. "Woohoo!"

What a thrill! He hadn't felt that way since...well, since he was *human*.

Tamping down his excitement, he pulled on the sail and steered them over the next wave.

Catheryn smiled at him as they worked together, him sailing them over the waves that were manageable, and her using her powers to help them go through the waves that weren't.

It was almost fun the way they were gliding through the storm.

"Look!" Catheryn said, pointing over Rainier's shoulder. "Is that…?"

"Land ho!" he shouted.

It was still several nautical miles away, and they had no way of knowing what the landform was or where they were, but it was better than being adrift at sea.

Rainier started to turn toward it, but then a wave came up suddenly next to them and crashed over them.

Catheryn screamed as she gripped her seat.

"Hold on!" Rainier said. "As we get closer to land, the waves get more dangerous."

Even though the waves were smaller, they rushed toward the land faster and harder, breaking as they crested. Rainier had a much more difficult time riding them than before.

"Catheryn," Rainier called out. "Forget about the land for now. We still have to steer through the waves."

She nodded and turned back to the sea, then waved her arms to try and separate them as before. But these waves were far less predictable. They seemed to come from nowhere. It was hard to tell what they were going to do.

When another one of the waves swooped up and crashed over the little boat, it knocked Catheryn off her feet. She slammed to the floor, hitting her chin.

"Catheryn," Rainier called, but he couldn't go to her side without letting go of the rigging.

Catheryn waved her hand. "I'm all right," she said, but her voice was winded. She must have been getting tired, which could also be why she was having difficulty controlling the waves.

"Hold on," Rainier said. "We will sail this out the old fashioned way." He tried to give her a reassuring wink.

Catheryn nodded, but her eyelids were heavy.

Rainier didn't have a good feeling about sailing through this, but he had no choice. He tried to turn the little ship into the waves as he had before, but they were rising so sharply, they nearly capsized. A wave fell over them again, filling the boat. They were going to sink.

Catheryn stood on wobbly legs.

"No, Catheryn," Rainier said. "Don't."

"I'm fine," she yelled back, her voice strained.

She held her hands up and groaned as she tried to part a way for them through the water, but it wasn't enough. The wave smashed onto the ship. Rainier shielded his face and held on tight. When he opened his eyes, Catheryn was gone.

Rainier stood. "Catheryn!"

His eyes frantically darted around the dark sea. Finally, he caught a glimpse of something. Her hand! But it was only there for a moment before it sank beneath the waves.

Rainier dove into the water and swam hard. The ocean under the surface was just as turbulent as it was up above. There were bubbles, seaweed, bits of wood, and other detritus being tossed to and fro beneath the waves. And it was still so dark. He could hardly see anything.

Rainier went back to the surface and took a deep breath. Then he dove back down again, swimming as deep as he could and looking left and right. As his eyes adjusted to the blackness of the water... There! There she was, sinking away from him.

He swam toward her, summoning the last of his vampiric strength. He reached, and finally he felt the tip of her fingers. He grasped hold and pulled her toward him. He was so weak, he could barely swim back to the top. He kicked and slowly they floated back toward the surface.

When they crested, he looked around. Their little boat was

gone, but the water was littered with bits of wood. He grabbed onto a plank of wood to buoy himself. He looked the other way and saw that the land they had seen before was much closer.

"Look, Catheryn. Land," he said. But she didn't respond.

Panic rose in his chest more violent than the worst of waves in any sea under any storm. He needed to get her to land.

With furious kicks, he propelled them toward shore. The sun was rising now, and the storm was abating. There was only a gentle shower falling on them. But the storm in his mind was even more furious than before.

Finally, after what seemed like hours of kicking but was probably only a few minutes, Rainier felt sand beneath his feet. He groggily walked toward the beach, the water getting more and more shallow.

"Catheryn, we made it," he said, a sinking feeling in his stomach when again she did not respond.

As he picked her up and carried her to the shore, she draped across his arms like dead weight.

Finally, he made it to dry land. He placed Catheryn down and patted her face. "Catheryn," he said gently. "Catheryn, wake up. We are here. We are safe now." He tapped her cheek. "Catheryn?"

Still nothing.

He placed his face next to her mouth, but she wasn't breathing.

CHAPTER 19

Catheryn...

Who's there? Catheryn asked.

Catheryn, the voice whispered again. The world was dark, but it was warm and comforting. She felt like she was floating.

Where am I? Catheryn asked. She wasn't using her voice, but seemed to be asking in her mind. Logically, she knew she needed to use her voice, but she was unable to, and speaking this way felt strangely natural.

Catheryn, I'm here...

Where? Catheryn asked, looking left and right. *Where are you? Who are you?*

Catheryn felt a gentle hand lightly touch her shoulder. She turned and saw a familiar face, one she hadn't seen in so long...

Don't you recognize me? the woman asked.

Eva! Catheryn said, grabbing her sister and puller her to her chest.

Fifteen years! It had been fifteen years since she had seen her little sister. Since that day she had sold herself into slavery to save her. Eva was a woman now, a beautiful woman with strong cheekbones and bright eyes, but the face of the child she knew was still there staring back at her.

I thought you were dead, Catheryn cried. *I hoped you were alive, and prayed you were, but without anyone to protect you, to raise you. Oh God! I feared the worst.*

Shhh... Eva cooed as she held her sister and stroked her hair. *Do not fear, sister. I am here now. You are safe.*

Am I? Catheryn asked. *Where am I? Am I...am I dead? Are you dead?*

Eva pulled away and stroked Catheryn's face. *No, we are not dead. You still have much work to do.*

What work? Catheryn asked. *What must I do? I've discovered these powers, but I have no idea what to do with them. Are you a hoodoo witch, too? Where are you? How can I find you?*

Eva took a step back, then another. Catheryn's vision started to blur and grow bright. *We will see each other again, sister...*

Wait! Catheryn screamed. *Don't leave me! Not again! I can't lose you! Eva! Eva...*

"Catheryn!" she heard a deeper voice say.

The light grew brighter. She felt heat and wet. She tried to open her eyes, but the sun was blinding.

"Catheryn! Come back to me!"

Rainier! She tried to speak, but could only cough. Seawater spilled from her mouth, and she gasped for air. Rainier held her tight.

"Thank God," Rainier said, pulling her into a sitting position and hugging her to his chest. "I thought I'd lost you."

Catheryn coughed and gasped a few more times. "You very nearly did," she finally sputtered. "I think I nearly headed for the great beyond."

"Are you all right?" he asked, running his hands over her arms, looking for injuries.

"I'm okay," she said with a weak smile. "I think I should be worried about you. Are you all right? You look like you just lost your best friend."

"Hmph," he said, pulling away a bit. "Well...if you had died, what would there be for me to eat?"

"Ouch," Catheryn said as she tried to get to her feet. "Didn't realize that's all I was to you."

"Sorry," he grumbled as he helped her up. "I just lost my ship, my crew, had to kill my best friend, thought you were dead, and am now stranded God knows where. It's been a taxing few hours."

"Well, thank you," she said, pulling him toward her. "For saving my life. Even if it's just to protect your next meal."

He smirked as he put his forehead against hers. "I think you've saved me a few times now as well. But who's keeping track?"

Catheryn pulled away, but she took his hand. She looked out to the sea. It was so calm now, you'd never know that a monster storm had nearly done them in. She looked down the beach one way, then the other. Behind them, there was only jungle.

"Any idea where we might be?" she asked.

"Well, the island where we found the wreckage was between Inagua and Abraham's Bay. However, I have a feeling that Mathis might have been steering us back to NOLA. If that's the case, he would have been sending us back to the Gulf. Considering how long we had been sailing, we are probably between Cuba and the Keys."

"There would be a lot of traffic through this area, then?" Catheryn asked. "Surely someone will sail by and could pick us up."

"Another vampire pirate ship?" Rainier asked. "You think we could trust another pirate crew after what just happened?"

"Well, we have to get off the island somehow," she said.

"What we have to do is find water, food, and shelter," Rainier said. He started stomping up the beach toward the jungle.

"Water and food, yes," Catheryn said, following him. "But we only need shelter if we plan to stay here."

"Are you planning on going somewhere?" he asked.

"We are surrounded by trees," she said. "We can just make another boat."

Rainier laughed. "What? You think trees just turn into boats? Unless you have some magical woodworking skills, I don't see that happening. I don't have any tools. I don't have any way to saw planks or sew a sail."

Catheryn wrinkled her nose, realizing he was right.

"What do you want to go back for anyway?" he asked. "The Hoodoo Queen just wants to make you her slave again."

"What's the alternative?" she asked.

Rainier shrugged as he started shimmying up a crooked palm tree. The tree was full of plantains. When he got to the top, he pulled out his sword and cut a bunch of the fruit free, which fell at Catheryn's feet. Rainier slid down the tree and joined her in digging into the delicious fruit.

"We could stay here," he said.

A bit of plantain caught in her throat, and she coughed. She looked at Rainier and saw sincerity in his eyes.

"You're serious," she said.

"Why wouldn't I be?"

Catheryn wasn't sure what to think about this. She stood and headed back to the beach. Stay on an island in the middle of the ocean with a vampire? It was crazy. She had to get back to civilization.

Didn't she?

"Catheryn," Rainier called after her. He followed her back to the beach, carrying a bunch of plantains. "Catheryn, what are you doing?"

"I...I don't know," she said. "I just can't imagine staying here...with you..."

"Why not?" he asked. "I'm not so awful, am I?"

"I never imagined a future with you in it before," she said. "You captured me. You fed from me. You're a vampire, a pirate. The idea that I would do anything but escape from you at some point never crossed my mind."

"Really?" Rainier asked, incredulously. He reached over and gently touched her face. "You never even fantasized about it?"

She felt a quivering in her belly as she recalled the night in his chambers when she almost gave herself to him. "Just because I wanted to sleep with you doesn't mean I wanted to spend the rest of my life with you."

Rainier smirked. "So you *did* want to sleep with me," he said. "And now? Do you still want to?"

She opened her mouth to say yes, but stopped herself. "We... we can't," she said. "I'm a witch. You're a vampire. And we sort of have bigger problems to worry about, being stranded on an island, in case you forgot!"

Rainier opened his arms. "Who is there here to judge us? Here, we are free to do as we please."

"And then what?" she asked. "After we give in, then what?"

"Then we...live happily ever after all alone on our secret island," he said.

"You need blood to live," she said. "You'll have to eat me eventually."

He nodded. "I have been feeling cravings," he said. "But I can control myself. I told you that as long as I don't kill you, you can build your blood back up. You can both live a long and healthy life and give me the sustenance I need."

"But what about..." Catheryn took a dep breath and shook her head.

"What about what?" he asked.

"Love," Catheryn said. "We don't love each other. Can we really live here, just the two of us for the rest of our lives? Wouldn't it be best if we get off this island and find our places in the world?"

Rainier walked up to Catheryn and took her face in his hands. He kissed her, more deeply and softly than she could have imagined. She leaned in and kissed him back.

"If you don't love me already," he whispered, "I'll make sure that one day you do."

Catheryn melted into him. She felt her knees go weak. Although she hadn't imagined a future with him in it, when she thought about it, she also couldn't imagine a future without him in it.

She pulled him down onto the sand, and he undid his sword belt, tossing it aside. When water from the rising tide tickled her toes, she realized for the first time that she wasn't wearing shoes. She must have lost them in the sea. But she didn't care. She was going to make love to her vampire and then stay with him here, forever.

Perhaps they'd both lost their minds at sea, but in this moment, she didn't care.

"Don't bite me," she said. "Every time you bite me, you pass out. I want you to take me."

He kissed her cheek, her throat. Then he licked her neck. "Every part of you tastes so good," he said, but he didn't bite her. He kissed down her chest and pulled open her shirt.

She gasped as the air ran across her breasts, followed by Rainier's mouth and tongue. The seawater splashed over them, but they didn't move from their spot.

Catheryn hiked up her skirt and removed her underwear. Rainier undid the buttons to his pants. Catheryn leaned back, ready for him.

Rainier paused. "You are sure?" he asked. "There's no going back after this."

Catheryn wasn't sure exactly what he meant—go back to NOLA? Go back to the way things were?—but she didn't care. She knew that this moment would change her for the rest of her life, but she just didn't care anymore. She wanted to have one good thing in her life—one pleasure.

"Yes," Catheryn said. "Please."

Rainier gripped her thigh and pulled her toward him. He

kissed her as he slid inside, and she moaned, wet with anticipation. As he thrust into her, he hooked his arm under one of her legs and lifted it, allowing him to enter her more deeply than any man before.

She arched her back as the waves of pleasure and of the sea washed over her and moaned her satisfaction as she held him tightly, her fingernails digging into his back. It was as if she couldn't hold him close enough as she reached the peak of delight.

His knees dug into the sand as he drove into her over and over again. "Catheryn!" he gasped as his climax came.

"Yes...yes..." she whispered as he pulsed within her.

When they were done, they both laid together in the sand, side by side, as waves rolling in from the sea washed them clean.

They finally managed to untangle themselves from each other, rinse the sand off themselves in the sea, and then continue exploring the island. Catheryn couldn't help but laugh to herself as Rainier went into provider and protector mode. They hadn't yet found fresh water, but he did find some coconuts and hacked one open for her so she could drink the fresh coconut milk.

"I've never been a fan of coconut," Catheryn said after her first swig, "but this is the most delicious thing I've ever tasted."

As they walked through the jungle, Rainier searched for a good place to build a shelter. With his sword, he hacked some large palm fronds free so they could use them as cover from the elements, but he was having issues finding anything to build a skeletal structure from.

"Is it part of being a pirate to have these sorts of survival skills?" Catheryn asked as she picked some berries.

"Certainly," Rainier said. "It's usually only a matter of time before you get marooned on an island. Either because of a storm or a mutiny or a sea battle. It's not usually a permanent situation, so you just have to make sure you survive long enough to get back to your ship or get picked up by another one."

Catheryn thought about this as they made their way to another section of beach. If was only a matter of time before another ship came by, what would they do? Would they hide? Would they go back? Would one of them stay and one of them go? What was there really waiting for them back in NOLA?

We will see each other again, sister...

Catheryn paused as the words of her dream came back to her. Surely it had just been a dream, right? She wouldn't really ever see Eva again, would she? It must have just been the desperate thoughts of a brain on the verge of death. If she was going to die, she would want to know that Eva was safe. That she had lived a long and healthy life. It was just her mind trying to comfort her as she nearly drowned.

Right?

She thought about the possibility of staying on the island forever with Rainier. After all, they had made love and the world hadn't ended. She wondered about the Rift that had shattered the world and created the Divisions. Most people said that it had been caused when a vampire and a witch had formed a forbidden pact. Many people assumed that part of the pact included the two making love. But now she wasn't so sure. Maybe her book...

Her book! It had been on the ship, and now it was probably lost forever. *Damn.* There was so much information in it. So much it could have still taught her.

Catheryn...

Catheryn thought she heard her name on the wind, but when she turned, she saw nothing.

"A boat!" Rainier called out, breaking Catheryn from her thoughts.

She looked up and saw Rainier running from down the beach. Sure enough, there was a small boat floating near a rocky outcropping. Catheryn walked down after him.

"It must have gotten caught in the rocks at low tide," Rainier said. He grabbed a rope and pulled the boat farther up into the sand. "Look at this," he said, reaching inside. "There are some tools here. The sail is a bit ratty, but that can probably be repaired. The oars look to be in surprisingly good condition…"

"So that's it then?" Catheryn asked, crossing her arms. "We were going to stay here forever but the first sign of a lifeboat and you're ready to go?"

Rainier walked over to her and put his arms around her. "I guess I just got excited," he said. "It's my natural inclination, to get back out on the sea. I'm a pirate, remember?"

"I remember," she said glumly.

"What do *you* want to do?" he asked. "I thought you didn't want to stay?"

Her gut was telling her they needed to leave the island, but she wasn't sure why. Was it just because people are taught to believe that they need to be around others? That they have to live in cities, or villages at least? Or was it because something was drawing her back? Eva? The Hoodoo Queen? Did she really want to go back? Or was she being manipulated somehow?

"I want to stay here with you," she said.

"But…?" Rainier asked, as though knowing there was more. *Catheryn…*

Catheryn closed her eyes and tried to shake the voice of her sister away, but she couldn't. *You still have much work to do…*

"But I feel like we need to go back. I don't know what it is. Should I ignore it? Should I answer it? You are right, we don't have anything to go back to. And I think we could be happy here, at least for a while. I don't know what to do."

Rainier frowned. "That's not a very clear response. But, if nothing else, we could use to boat for fishing, until you do decide what you want to do. We can get better fish if we get away from the coast."

"I wish we'd never found this boat," Catheryn mumbled.

Rainier folded his arms across his chest. "Why?"

"I was just imagining that we would stay here, happy together alone. But now that we have a means to leave, I feel like I need to return to NOLA."

"Return to NOLA?" he asked. "Just because you want to leave the island doesn't mean you have to return to NOLA. The Hoodoo Queen will find you right away. We can go anywhere. Why do you want to go back to NOLA?"

"I don't know," Catheryn said. She didn't want to tell him about her vision of Eva. He would tell her she was crazy to be putting so much stock into the images of a delirious brain on the brink of death. And he would be right. "But something—someone —is calling me, telling me I need to go back."

CHAPTER 20

Rainier slaved away in the hot sun as he worked on the boat. He couldn't believe that Catheryn was even *considering* going back to NOLA. For the first time since he met Catheryn, he felt a sense of freedom. He didn't have to worry about his vampire powers fading, his growing unrest with the crew, the rising tides sending the humans inland, their seemingly foolish quest to find a way to access another Division...

He sighed. He loved being a pirate, sailing the seas. Feeling the gentle rock of the ship beneath his feet. Watching the stars at night. But lately, the stress of it all had been wearing him down, even before he met Catheryn. Catheryn...well, she just complicated matters further.

He didn't want to give her up. He had chosen her over his crew. Could he ever hope to build up another crew after he had betrayed his previous one and killed his first mate? If any of his mates survived, they would tell everyone what happened. His reputation would be ruined. No one would sail with him again. If the crew all drowned, that would be even worse. The lone survivor of the shipwreck was the captain? He'd never live down the shame of it.

No, he had to stay here. There was nothing for him any longer out there in the wide world. This island was the only future he had. At least here, he could live in peace.

He could live with Catheryn. If she'd stay. He would have to convince her.

He watched as Catheryn sat on the beach, staring out at the sea. She was so beautiful. Surely she didn't really want to go back. She felt obligated to help others; it was just her nature because she was a good person. But he had to help her see that she didn't owe those people anything. She could stay here, too. She had a right to peace and happiness as well. She could find it here, with him.

He whistled, and Catheryn looked at him. They smiled at each other. She stood up and dusted the sand off her legs as she wandered over to help hold a plank tight while he secured it. They worked together in companionable silence for a few minutes before Rainier finally spoke.

"So, ever made love in the sand before?" he asked.

She blushed. "No. I think I'll be digging sand out of my nether regions for weeks."

They both laughed. Rainier was surprised at how easily they talked and worked together. There was no awkwardness like what he usually experienced with lovers the hours after.

"I know you feel like you have to go back," he finally said. The smile ran away from her face. "But you do have a choice. You don't have to go."

"Are you serious?" she asked. "You think we can just stay here on this island for the rest of our lives? What would that look like?"

"Well, I have a few ideas," he said. "First, we need to keep exploring. There is no telling what useful items we might find. It's possible other people have been stranded here before and left things behind. We will probably find more washed up items as well. But with these tools, I can start fashioning a shelter, once the boat is done."

"What kind of shelter?" she asked. "Some palm fronds draped over sticks?"

"I was thinking something more like a log cabin, but made out of palm trees," he said. "You saw the types of homes the people had built in that village we attacked. They actually aren't that difficult to construct with the right tools and the right know-how."

"And you have the right know-how?" She crossed her arms and smirked.

"You know the great thing about a new relationship is that everything about me is new and surprising again," he said. "I get to impress you with all the things I know how to do. I can regale you with stories my crew had heard a hundred times. Not to mention you might find all my jokes funny."

"I've never heard you tell a joke," she said. "Tell me one. Make me laugh."

Rainier screwed up his face as he thought. "Why does it take a pirate so long to learn the alphabet?"

"I don't know," Catheryn said. "Why *does* it take so long for a pirate to learn the alphabet?"

"Because they can spend years at C."

Catheryn stared at him a moment before she finally threw her head back and laughed. It was a melodic tinkling sound. Rainier chuckled, relieved she found his joke funny, and kept working.

"That was really terrible," she finally said.

"Well, there's a million more where that came from," he replied. "I can't wait to tell you all of them."

"A million, huh?" she asked of no one in particular. "So, this is it, you think? This is what you want? Fix this fishing boat, build a little house, then just live happily ever after?"

Rainier nodded. "It's not too bad of a dream, is it?"

"Is it what you really want?" she asked. "I seem to recall you telling me about how happy you were at sea."

"That's a fair question," he said. "I lived my whole life at sea. I never imagined there was any other way to live. At least, not until you came along."

Their eyes met. How he longed to know what she was thinking in that moment. Her face softened, and he thought he saw tears well up. A surge of warmth welled up in his chest. He put his tools down, walked over to her, and held her in his arms while she squeezed him tightly.

"I release you," he whispered.

She pulled back a bit and looked him in the eyes. "What?"

"I release you," he repeated. "You are no longer my slave, my devotee. I know it might not mean much out here." He waved his arm toward the long and empty beach. "But I want you to stay. And I want you to want to stay. I want to know you are choosing to be here with me."

Catheryn stood up on her tiptoes and kissed him, gently yet eagerly. "Thank you for that," she said. "That means more to me than you know." She stepped away from him and pulled the straps of her dress over her shoulders. The dress slid down her body, leaving her naked on the beach.

"This is the first time in longer than I can remember that I am a free woman," she said. "This is the first decision I've made that is completely unencumbered by the fact that someone else owns me."

"And what decision is that?" he asked, feeling his manhood grow hard.

She opened her arms to him. "Let's make love in the ocean."

She didn't have to tell him twice. He quickly threw off his clothes and together they ran into the warm surf. The sun was setting now, giving off an orange glow. They held hands as they walked out into the water deep enough that it came to Rainier's chest. She wrapped her legs around his waist and her arms around his neck. He entered her quickly and easily. With every thrust, her full breasts bounced in and out of the water. They were mesmerizing as Rainier watched. Catheryn tossed her head back, and her dark tresses floated freely on top of the water. He watched her face as she climaxed, the way her mouth opened wide in pleasure. He held her tightly as he spilled into her, and he didn't want to let her go.

He carried her back to land and together they laid in the sand to dry, and there they stayed, watching as the stars appear.

As they snuggled, Rainier felt a wave of exhaustion crash over him. He knew what it meant. It had been too long since he last fed. The plantains would not sustain him. Even though he worried that feeding off Catheryn was causing his vampire powers to fade, he was still vampire, and he had to drink at least some human blood to survive. If he didn't, he would slip into a torpor state and eventually die. He hated that he had to ask to feed off her after they had connected in such a way, a new way of trust, love, and respect, but he had no choice.

"Catheryn," he said softly.

"Hmm?"

"I...I need to feed," he said. "I hate to admit it, but I do."

Catheryn didn't move or say anything for a moment, and for a second he feared she would refuse. After all, as a free woman, she could say no.

"Do you really think my blood is causing you to lose your vampire powers?" she asked.

"I can't think of any other explanation," he said. "I didn't have any of these symptoms—these changes—until I started feeding from you."

"Could you really live like that?" she asked. "You have already given up on being a pirate. Could you give up on being a vampire, too?"

"I...I don't know," he said. "I hadn't really thought about it. So much has happened lately, and I've been spending so much time thinking about the changes you are going through, I hadn't considered the changes I was facing..."

No longer be a vampire? Was it even possible? Being a vampire was who he was. It wasn't just a life he chose. There was no "cure," and he never had imagined there needed to be one. Being a vampire wasn't an illness, no matter what the witches or humans thought. He knew that feeding off Catheryn was weakening him, but actually turning him...what? Human? Impossible! If he went back to feeding on normal humans, his vampire strength would return, he was sure of it.

"Don't worry," he said. "I'm sure my strength will return at some point. Eventually another ship will come by or some poor soul will wash up on the shore. If I can drink pure human blood again, I am sure that someday my full vampire powers will return. I just need to drink from you for now, to get me by."

Catheryn seemed to hesitate. He wasn't sure why, but he was afraid to ask. He didn't think he would like the answer. If she didn't want him to return to being a vampire, could they really be together? If she couldn't love him as a vampire, could he love her if he was human?

That was a possibility he didn't want to face.

He had a feeling she didn't either because she didn't ask him anything further. She simply nodded and turned her head away, exposing her neck.

He leaned over her and kissed her neck gently. He caressed her body and felt her arousal grow again. As her heart rate increased, he could see the pulse beat more strongly, more quickly. He licked his lips, and then his fangs descended as he went in for the bite.

Catheryn gasped and gripped him tightly. Her blood spurted into his mouth, and he drank it eagerly. She wrapped her leg around him, holding him closer, and she moaned. He gripped the back of her head as he sucked deeply from her. God, she tasted so good.

A light flashed. He looked up. Standing before him was the Hoodoo Queen. She was on the porch of the Hoodoo House. She was giving orders to people. As he looked around, he saw his crewmates in chains. The witches were herding them toward the slave quarters behind the house. Rainier got up and ran to them.

"Men!" he cried out. "What is going on? Why aren't you fighting back?"

But they didn't answer. It was as if they couldn't see him. He reached out and shook one of them by the shoulder, but he didn't respond. It was only then that he realized he was having another vision. But this seemed so much more real, more concrete. As if it was really happening.

He ran up the line of shackled men to the slave quarters. From inside, he heard screaming, and then silence. One after another, a man was led through the doors and never seen again. Rainier ran back down the line and realized that there were too many people. These weren't only his crewmen who were being killed. There were many humans chained along with them, and vampires he didn't know.

He ran back to the front of the house. The Hoodoo Queen was surrounded by her acolytes.

"Soon, my darlings. Soon NOLA will be cleansed. There is no need or place for humans in this perfect world. They exist only to feed the vampires, and vampires only to feed from humans. We have no need of either. No human or vampire will find safety or succor here in my Division. There will be only witch-kind here. Then finally we will be able to repair this broken world. We will unite the Divisions. We will fix what the vampires shattered."

"No!" Rainier said. "I will stop you. I will make sure you pay for this wickedness you have wrought."

The queen laughed. "You? Who are you? You are nothing. Just a weak vampire without a ship. Just stay on your pathetic island, alone. No one will miss you, and no one will weep for you when you are dead."

"You are not as powerful as you think," he said. "Catheryn is stronger. You are afraid of her power. She will stop you."

The Hoodoo Queen narrowed her eyes at him. "Where are

you?" she asked. "I can see the trees, the water, the little boat. I know you are marooned. But where?" She reached out a hand toward him, and black shadows seemed to reach from her fingertips toward him. "I see you," she whispered harshly. "I will find you... Eventually, Rainier Dulocke, I will find you, and I will kill you."

CHAPTER 21

Catheryn laid in the sand, watching the stars and listening to the surf as she held Rainier in her arms. He had passed out once again, but she was growing used to it. Hopefully he would be stronger when he woke and have a clear head so they could decide the way forward together.

Had she really just made love to a vampire? Twice? In all her days, she never imagined she would end up in the arms of a vampire. Did she really want to stay here with him?

Yes. She did want to stay and build a little house and go fishing and climb trees and live a simple life with him. But...

But what she wanted to do and what she *needed* to do were two different things. Ever since Rainier took her from the Hoodoo House, her world had changed. Nothing was simply coincidence. The visions she and Rainier had been having were more than just dreams. The vision of her sister—it had to be more than just the addles of a drowning brain.

The prospect of a simple life with Rainier was beautiful, but she knew her powers had to mean more than that. She was the last pure blood hoodoo witch. She couldn't let her powers go to waste on catching fish and cracking coconuts.

But was she really the last hoodoo witch? If her powers manifested late in life, maybe Eva's did, too. Maybe that was how Eva had managed to reach out to her.

Catheryn's heart beat fast. It had been so long since she had seen her sister, that she had given up hope of ever seeing her again. But as she thought about how she could use her powers to find her sister, tears came to her eyes. The Hoodoo Queen had reached out to Catheryn and talked to her through the mirror. Eva had called to her when she was in the sea. It had to be possible for Catheryn to reach out as well. She needed to call out to Eva. They needed to find each other...

"Ahhh!" Rainier gasped and coughed as he sat up, thumping his chest.

"Are you all right?" Catheryn asked, propping herself up on her elbows.

Rainier looked at her, his eyes wide and his face paler than usual. "Sure. Sure. I'm fine."

He stumbled down to the water and splashed his face.

Catheryn followed him. "Are you sure?".

He washed up a bit more and then nodded his head. "Yeah. I'm fine. I'm fine."

Catheryn crossed her arms. He was obviously not fine. When he drank from her in the past, he had visions. He must have had another one—one that upset him greatly.

When she didn't say anything, he finally glanced up at her.

"What?" he asked.

"I'm just giving you time to process whatever you saw before you tell me," she said.

"I didn't see anything," he said. "Just, you know, your blood always leaves me feeling...weird."

"Usually because you have a vision," Catheryn said. "Tell me."

"Look, it's nothing," he said again, more firmly this time. He stood up and turned away from her, heading back toward the boat.

Catheryn's heart sped faster. "Don't lie to me, Rainier," she said. "We are supposed to be in this together. I can't trust you if you won't tell me the truth."

"Will you stay?" he asked, turning back to her.

"What do you mean?" she asked.

"Will you stay with me, here on the island, if I tell you?"

Catheryn's hands dropped to her side. "I can't promise that. I don't know what you saw."

"Then I'm not going to tell you," he said.

Catheryn felt a strength burst forth from her chest. He was not going to keep secrets from her and try to control her. She stomped forward and grabbed his shoulder. She turned him around and pushed him up against the boat with a preternatural strength beyond what he possessed in his weakened state.

"Tell me!" she said firmly. "If you don't tell me, I'll leave anyway because I'll not stay with someone who would keep secrets to try and manipulate me."

"Fine!" Rainier yelled.

She let him go, and he straightened his coat.

"Fine. You want to know?" he asked, his glare hitting her own gaze with the sharpness of a dagger. "That bitch queen is rounding up anyone in NOLA who isn't a witch and is killing them."

Catheryn reeled back and put her hands to her mouth.

"The vampires and the humans," he said. "She's going to kill them all. She called it a great cleansing."

"No," Catheryn said. "We have to go back. We have to stop her."

"Why?" Rainier asked. "How? You can't control your powers. Your blood has left me a shell of the vampire I once was. What have the people of NOLA ever done for us? Stay here, Catheryn. Stay. We can live in peace here."

"Peace?" Catheryn asked. "You could live in peace knowing what is happening not far from here? Knowing that thousands of people are being exterminated? Besides, after she is done cleansing the mainland, what is to stop her from coming to the islands? To keep her from coming after us? We can stop her before it's too late. While there are still people to save."

Rainier shook his head, and a bitter smile overtook his features. "Yeah, we should have known better than to even pretend we could have a future together."

"What's that supposed to mean?" Catheryn asked, trying to steel herself against his cutting words.

"You're a witch. I'm a vampire. We can't be together," he said. "I can't turn you into a vampire. Witches can't be turned. And I'm still a vampire, even if I am weak. I can feel it in the deepest parts of me. I am vampire."

"We were still witch and vampire when we were talking about forever," Catheryn said. "That hasn't changed."

"We were just being stupid. Foolish. We can't ignore our basic instincts."

"We can still be together," Catheryn said. "Come with me back to NOLA. Fight with me. If we win, if we stop her, then we can come back here and live in peace."

"That will never happen," Rainier said.

"Why not?"

"Mainly because we *won't* win," he said. "You have these innate powers, but they are still new, still raw, still untrained. She might have learned her craft, but she has honed it well. And she has the most powerful, most well-trained coven in the Division. You can't fight all of them. If we go back, we will die."

Catheryn let out an exasperated sigh. "Where is this coming from?" she asked. "Why are you so defeated?"

"I'm just a realist," he said. "It is something you learn as captain. When to take risks and when to fall back. I'm telling you, as a strategist, you need to pull back."

"I can't do that," she said. "So come up with a new strategy."

Rainier laughed. "It doesn't work like that," he said. "When the odds are against you, there's no point to it."

"Then stay," she said. "Build your little hut and catch your little fish and just stay here. I'll go alone."

Rainier gripped her wrist. "And you wonder why I didn't want to free you. It's been barely an hour, and already you are running off."

"Why shouldn't I?" Catheryn asked, her glare dropping to his hand.

"Because…because I love you." They both stood in silence for a moment. His grip on her wrist loosened, and then he let her go.

"What?" Catheryn finally managed to ask.

"You heard me," he said. "You can't tell me you don't feel the same."

"I…I don't know," she said. "I've never been in love before. And…and I can't think about this!" She took a few steps back, putting some distance between them, moving herself closer to the boat. "People are dying, Rainier. This isn't just about *us*."

"What people?" Rainier asked, a dark storm in his eyes. "Pirates? Strangers? People who'd no sooner see you dead? Why do you care?"

"Because my sister is out there," Catheryn said. Tear flooded her eyes. Tears she didn't have time to cry.

"What?" Rainier asked.

"My sister, Eva," she said, her voice nearly a choked whisper now. "I told you about her. She's out there. She's alive. She's calling to me."

"What do you mean?" Rainier stepped closer, but Catheryn stepped back again. "What are you talking about?"

"When I was drowning," Catheryn said, "she came to me. She said I still had work to do, that we would meet again."

"Why didn't you tell me?" He didn't advance on her again. Just reached his arm toward her, then let it float back to his side.

"I...I wasn't sure it was real. I thought I was dying. But it was so clear. I saw her face. Felt her hand. And ever since I woke up, I can't get her out of my mind. I can hear her; her voice is calling to me."

Rainier ran his hand over his jaw. "Yeah..." he mumbled.

"What?" Catheryn asked.

"What did she look like?" he asked. "When you saw her?"

"I...I don't know," Catheryn said. "The vision was...abstract. It was dark, but I could feel her. I knew she was there before I saw her... And when I did see her, through the darkness, she looked sort of like me. We were close in age. She was wearing all white, like an angel. But her hair. It was cut short, really short."

Rainier nodded. "I saw her," he said. "In one of my visions."

This time, Catheryn stepped toward him. "Why didn't you tell me?"

"It was a while back. When I woke, you were asleep, so I slipped out of the room. I forgot to tell you later. I thought it was you I saw, but there was something not quite right about you. The face I saw was not quite the same and the hair was short."

Catheryn urged him on with a roll of her hand. "Okay, and? Tell me more. Tell me what happened."

"She was leading an assault on the Hoodoo House."

Catheryn felt the world spin. She stared past Rainier, into the shadows between the trees, and shook her head. "She can't," she whispered. "She could be killed. She can't do that."

"You could be killed, *too*," Rainier said, gripping her shoulders. "Catheryn, think with your brain and not with your heart for just one moment. This whole thing is madness."

"I have to go back," Catheryn said. "My sister needs me. Even if I didn't care about anyone else in NOLA, I have to go back for her."

Rainier sighed and stepped back. "Well, I'll not help you," he said. "If you go, you go on your own."

"I thought you loved me," she said.

"I do," he said, turning away from her.

At this angle, it almost looked as if...as if a tear was sliding down his face. But before Catheryn could be sure, he turned further away.

"And that's why I can't go," he said. "I can't watch you be killed."

"Then help me," she said. "I need you. I need someone I can trust. Someone who will have my back."

Rainier shook his head.

"I'll not come back," she said. "If you go with me and we survive, we will be together. I'll come live on this silly island with you until I die. But if you don't go and I live, I'll not come back. I wouldn't be able to look you in the face."

"Love or life, Catheryn," he said. "Which do you think a pirate would choose?"

Catheryn felt her heart sink. She had never been so disgusted with another person. He was being cowardly. *Some pirate.* She shook her head, unable to believe what he was saying.

"You are not the man I thought you were, Rainier Dulocke," she said.

He shrugged. "Then you must have never known the real me."

How childish! Catheryn though, overcome by hurt and anger. She ground her teeth together and reached her hand out toward the back of his head.

"Sleep," she whispered.

"What the..." Rainier started to turn back to face her, but as his body twisted, he fell to the sand.

"Thanks for fixing the boat," she said as he passed out.

Catheryn walked over and pushed the little boat into the water, then jumped in and tossed the tools out onto the ground. She didn't know much of anything about sailing aside from what she had seen Rainier do earlier, but she hoped it was enough. She unfurled the sail and tied it taught. Then she blew out into the sail.

"Take me to NOLA," she whispered.

The wind gently picked up and carried her out to sea. She watched as the little island faded from view. It was a pretty dream, the one Rainier had of them living on it safely, peacefully for the rest of their days. But that's all it was. A dream. The visions she had been having since her powers started manifesting were so much more. The task before her was bigger than she was, it was bigger than Rainier, and it was bigger than the two of them together.

She had to go back, even if it meant leaving the man she loved behind forever.

CHAPTER 22

Rainier sat on the beach and watched the sunrise. *Get ready for a lot of lonely mornings*, he thought to himself. He couldn't believe she left. And that she took the boat. Well, actually he could. How did he think she was going to get off the island? At least she left him the tools. He might be able to build another boat. If he lived that long. Did she realize that, by leaving, she had sentenced him to death? How would he survive without blood?

He sighed as the waves lapped at his toes. She had been right to leave. He had acted like a coward. He didn't think he was being cowardly, though. Just pragmatic. Going back was suicide. But it probably looked like cowardice to her. Why couldn't she see he was only trying to protect her? He loved her and wanted to keep her safe.

He nearly laughed out loud. He couldn't believe he told her he loved her. It was true, but he shouldn't have admitted such a thing. It made him look weak, and now was when he needed to be strong. The Hoodoo Queen was dangerous, and she was killing anyone and anything that stood in her path. If Catheryn decided to fight against her instead of allying with her, Catheryn wouldn't stand a chance.

"Damnit," he muttered.

He had to help her. He should have gone with her. He knew she would go, with or without him. He should have gotten in the damn boat!

Rainier narrowed his eyes as something came into view. There was something floating on the water, heading toward the island. A boat!

"Hey!" he yelled, waving his arms. "Over here!" He jumped up and down, hoping the boat's owner would see him. As the boat floated nearer, though, he realized there was no owner. It was *his* boat. The one he had repaired. The one Catheryn had stolen.

He couldn't help but laugh out loud. Catheryn had sent the boat back. Maybe she did love him too.

But if she'd used her magic to send the boat back, that meant she'd reached NOLA. And if she'd reached NOLA, alone, then she was in danger.

~

He could hear the city before he could see it. The music, the laughter, the sounds of thousands of people in one of the oldest cities in the Division.

It was late, the moon in full bloom above the shore, but the city was lit up like noon. Shops and homes and streetlamps all burned brightly. Rainier pulled up at one of the city's countless docks and walked freely among the throngs of people.

For a city that could soon be facing extermination, everyone sure seemed chipper. People were going about their daily lives, drinking, dancing, shopping like they didn't have a care in the world. But that was NOLA for you. The people here loved life.

He walked past a restaurant where the spice wafted out the window and just begged you to go inside. Like most cities, the population of NOLA mostly lived separate lives, with witches, vampires, and humans occupying different communities. But there was another side to NOLA as well—the Mardi Gras Coast, what was left of the former French Quarter.

In the Mardi Gras, all of the races mixed freely. It was a dangerous place, with skirmishes breaking out with fair regularity. Drugs, sex, black-market goods—anything could be bought and sold in the Mardi Gras. But it was also where a person could hide, blend in with the throngs of unwashed souls. If Catheryn had returned but didn't want the queen to find her, this is where she would hide.

"Tell your fortune, deary?" a young woman on a street corner asked Rainier as he passed. He smiled at her but shook his head.

"Maybe there is something else you'd rather buy?" a woman standing next to her asked as she ran her fingers over her amble breasts seductively.

Rainier shook his head again.

"Or *someone* else?" a svelte young man suggested, rubbing up against him.

Rainier smiled and tossed the man a coin. "There is someone I'm looking for," he said. "A young witch, dark skin, long hair. Goes by the name of Catheryn."

The young fellow ran the coin between his fingers, then it miraculously disappeared. "Can't say that I've seen her. But if you want any information about anyone, I'd check in the Bawdy Wench—the tavern up the road. Barnaby there knows anything you'd want to ask."

"Thanks, friend," Rainier said.

"Anything you need, handsome," the young man replied, followed by a playful air kiss.

Rainier shook his head as he walked away and headed toward the tavern.

The tavern was as lively as ever. The drinks were flowing. People were playing games of chance. There were plenty of prostitutes—male, female, vampire, witch, and human. If there was anywhere on earth all people lived together in harmony, it was in a tavern.

Rainier sidled up to the bar and ordered a drink.

"As I live and breathe!" a familiar female voice said as a smooth hand slid its way over his shoulder. "Rainier Dulocke."

"Rene," Rainier said, removing her hand from his person and resting his hand on his sword.

"Now, now," she said, pouting. "Is that any way to greet me?"

"Nice to see you've managed to dry yourself off," he said.

"Oh, you know me," she said. "I was made to be wet." She licked her lips.

Rainier rolled his eyes. "What are you doing here, Rene?"

"Normally I'd get mad at you for not speaking to me captain to captain," she said. "You never could accept that I was your equal. But you aren't a captain anymore, are you?"

Rainier took a swig from his glass. "What do you know about it?"

She shrugged. "I know your men sailed into port without you. Well, limped into port is more like it. Not sure how they made it with their ship in that condition. I know they had thrown you overboard after you killed your first mate. I know your men marched straight up to the Hoodoo House like they had some urgent business. And I know they haven't been seen since."

"They didn't throw me overboard," he said into his cup.

"Oh, of course not," she said. "You jumped over to save your lady love. Is that your version?"

Rainier looked at her but didn't reply. She just stared back with a goofy grin on her face. "And I know the Hoodoo Queen is looking for you."

Rainier gulped his drink down. "Is she paying you to deliver me?"

"Not me," she said. "I'd never betray a fellow vampire, even one as repulsive as you, to a witch."

Rainier eyed her, not sure if he could trust her words.

"I was always a better pirate and a better vampire than you, Rainier. Even if you don't want to admit it. Consider this fair warning on two counts. Firstly, that the queen is looking for you. So watch your back."

"And secondly?" he asked.

"If you find yourself on a ship again, I'll sink it," she said. "I wouldn't be so uncouth as to run you through on dry land. But if you find yourself at sea again, I'll kill you."

"I look forward to seeing you soon then, *Captain* Lacroix," he said, toasting her with his mug.

"Sweet talker," she said before walking out of the tavern, a group of her men behind her.

"What a woman," the bartender said as he watched Rene leave appreciatively. "Can I top you off, sir?" he asked, turning to Rainier.

Rainier handed him his glass. "Sure thing. Been a long time since I've had a good ale."

"I thank you, sir," he said as he filled the glass.

"Are you the one they call Barnaby?" Rainier asked.

"Aye, that's me," he said. "What can I do ya for?"

"I heard you are the man who knows things," Rainier said.

The bartender shrugged as he wiped down the bar. "People get chatty when they drink. I'm a good listener. It is what it is."

"I'm looking for someone. A young woman."

The bartender's cleaning slowed a bit. "Lots of young women here," he said. "We have one for every taste..." He motioned to the prostitutes across the room.

"Not that kind of woman," Rainier said, annoyed. "Catheryn Beauregard. A young witch. She would be looking for a girl named Eva."

The room got noticeably quieter, and the bartender's head beaded with sweat. "You must be Captain Dulocke."

"I am," Rainier said, not seeing a reason to hide it.

"I don't want no trouble," the bartender said, his eyes darting around. Rainier could feel some of the other patrons moving in closer.

"I'm not here to cause any," Rainier said, his senses coming alive. "I'm just looking for the girl."

"She's not here," the bartender said. "But she was. She was seen heading west on Dauphine."

Dauphine? Rainier thought to himself. *West?* That would be toward the Hoodoo House. She wasn't thinking about heading straight there, was she? She wouldn't be that stupid. She said she was going to look for her sister, Eva. She would need help if she was going to confront the queen.

The bartender's eyes opened as he stepped back, and Rainier ducked to the side just as a wooden club crashed down onto the bar. Rainier turned and grabbed the man who had just tried to bash his head in. He slammed the man's head into a barstool.

Then Rainier turned and saw that he was surrounded. Four men came at him at once. Thankfully Rainier had fed just before Catheryn fled, so he still had some strength and some of his vampire vigor. The men swung at him with their fists and with swords and wooden stakes, but he bested them all, seamlessly gliding from one to the other. A snap of the neck there, a punch to the gut here. It was like a dance, if one of the dancers ended up dead as the climax. It was a dance Rainier had missed performing.

After he was done, Rainier stood panting. The other patrons stood back, horrified. Rainier wiped the blood off his face and tossed the barkeep a gold coin.

"For the damage," he said.

Then he stomped out the door and headed down Dauphine.

It was now getting into the wee hours of the morning, and the people were finally quieting down and heading to their homes or wherever they were planning to sleep for a few hours before the day began.

Rainier couldn't believe he was heading to the Hoodoo House.

He was just as crazy as Catheryn was, or at least crazy for her. He'd follow her anywhere, though, even if it was into the jaws of death.

Rainier heard a few steps behind him—the soft, light steps of a woman. He turned.

"Catheryn?" he called out, but he saw nothing.

He turned back, but he could feel his senses tingling. It wasn't the warning sense of a bunch of clumsy humans like back at the bar, but the acute subtle sense you get when you know something is wrong.

A shadow blinked up ahead. He looked to the side, but saw only a black cat leap away. Then he heard a soft giggling. They were coming for him.

Witches.

He wasn't sure if they were in the thrall of the Hoodoo Queen or from a rival coven, but it didn't seem to matter. Both were equally bad options.

In a puff of black smoke, a woman appeared in front of him. He quickly drew his cutlass and sliced across her belly, but the sword went right through her like she wasn't even there. She laughed. Then he heard more laughter.

Once again, he was surrounded.

He hacked at them, one and then the other, but his sword had no effect. They moved in closer, and black smoke enveloped him. It went down his throat and pinned his arms to his sides.

Rainier fell to his knees, chocking all the while.

CHAPTER 23

Catheryn avoided the busy parts of the city, but that was hard to do. The city was alive, teeming with people. But she had not been in NOLA proper since she was sold into slavery and entered the Hoodoo House. She hoped that no one would recognize her or know who she was.

She had no plan as she walked the dark streets. What was she doing here? Was she just going to waltz up to the queen and demand she stop killing people? She should have waited for Rainier to change his mind. He would have come around eventually. He wouldn't really just sit on the sidelines on his little island and let people die.

Would he?

She didn't think so. But if he did, he certainly wasn't the kind of man she wanted in her life. She would be better off without him. Or she would be dead. At least then it wouldn't matter.

Catheryn sighed and shook her head. This was going to be a disaster.

If only she could find Eva. Then she would have at least one ally in the city. She was certain Eva was alive, but she had no idea where she was or how to find her. She might not even use the name Eva anymore. What if she wasn't in NOLA? The Division was huge, encompassing most of the southeast of what was the United States and the Caribbean Islands, which were too numerous to count. She could be anywhere.

Catheryn's walk slowed. This was a fool's errand. She needed a better plan. She should go back to Rainier. He was the only person she knew who could help her. Together they could formulate a better plan.

But she had sent the little boat back to him, so he wouldn't be left stranded. He would have starved if she hadn't, but now that left her stuck. How would she get back without a boat? She couldn't buy one because she didn't have any money. Well, she did still have the coin with her ancestral symbol on it, but she couldn't part with that. She'd have to steal a boat.

She shook her head. She always turned to thievery in a pinch, though it usually caused her more trouble in the end.

She turned to head back to the waterfront, but as she did, she saw a shadow move. Her breath hitched in her throat. Was she being followed?

Her eyes darted from side to side. She didn't see anyone else, but she had that sickening feeling she wasn't alone, that she was being watched.

She took a few steps, but heard an echo. It almost sounded like her own footsteps echoing off the walls, but it was too far away, too distinct. She took another step and heard it again. Someone was definitely following her, and trying to mask their steps. Was it the Hoodoo Queen, or some of her acolytes?

If the queen had been able to find her in the middle of the ocean, she should have no problem finding Catheryn here, on home turf.

Catheryn's heart thudded faster in her chest. She was just about to run when a hand fell over her mouth. She tried to yell, to raise her arms and use her magic to defend herself, but the person was holding a rag dipped in something foul-smelling.

Catheryn opened her mouth to scream.

Instead, she passed out.

Catheryn felt warm, as though she was wrapped in a safe blanket. The smell of food filled her nose. She couldn't remember the last time she woke up feeling safe and cared for. Afraid she was still dreaming, she didn't want to open her eyes, but slowly, she did.

Sitting beside her was a hooded woman. Catheryn started and sat up straight. She was in a large room lit with candles. There were many people there, watching her. On one side of the room, a woman was stirring a large pot of stew. Catheryn's mouth watered. How long had it been since she'd eaten?

"Who are you?" Catheryn asked the hooded woman. "Why am I here?"

"You are Catheryn?" the woman asked, something familiar about that voice. "The woman who was a slave?"

"Yes," Catheryn said. "I was a slave in the Hoodoo House for fifteen years before I was kidnapped by vampire pirates. I escaped and came back here." She figured she should keep the part about sleeping with the Rainier and then abandoning him on the island to herself for now.

"Why did you come back?" the woman asked.

"To find my sister," she said. "We were separated as children, but I am sure she is alive."

The hooded woman shuddered. Catheryn thought maybe she was crying.

"What...what was your sister's name?" the woman asked.

"Eva," Catheryn said.

The woman nodded and pulled the hood back. Catheryn saw the face from her dream.

"Eva!" Catheryn called out. She pulled her sister into her arms and the two wept together. Catheryn held Eva's face in her arms and kissed her cheeks. "I can't believe it's you!"

"I know," Eva said. "I've been looking for you all these years. Forgive me for the secrecy and cloak and dagger routine, but I needed to make sure you were really Catheryn and not one of the Hoodoo Queen's spies."

"It's fine. It's fine. I've been in the Hoodoo House the whole time," Catheryn said. "After I went with the slave trader, he took me to the auction house and the queen bought me. I was there until only a few weeks ago when she gave me to the vampire pirates."

Eva shook her head. "That bitch. Did she know she was sentencing you to death after so many years of faithful service?"

"I don't think she cared," Catheryn said. "At least not at the time."

Eva nodded. "I finally figured out you had been in the Hoodoo House when the queen started looking for you. She put a price on your head, you and the pirate Rainier."

"Does she know I've returned?"

"I don't know," Eva said. "But why did you? You should have known it's not safe here."

"I came to find you," Catheryn said. "You called to me. I saw you in a vision, when I nearly drowned. You said that my work wasn't done and that we would see each other again."

Eva laughed, as did several of her friends. "I think it was the lack of oxygen trying to keep you alive."

"No," Catheryn said. "Aren't you...aren't *we*...you know...?"

"What?" Eva asked.

"Aren't you a...a pure blood witch? Like me?"

Eva's eyebrows pulled together. "You're a pure blood witch? What do you mean?"

Catheryn sighed. "It's a long story, but do you remember our parents at all?"

Eva shook her head.

"Apparently they were the last of pure blood hoodoo witches. As their children, we could be the last pure blood witches in the Division."

"You're a witch?" Eva asked.

"And so are you," Catheryn said. "We have the same parents. And I saw you in my vision. Rainier, he saw you, too. You must be a witch."

Another woman, an older one, spoke up as she brought over a bowl of stew and some fresh bread. "Old world magic? Fickle, it is. Not all children of witches inherit the gift. Not all witches have witch parents. Witchcraft can be innate or learned. That's why the pure bloods died out. It was unpredictable. It wasn't something that could always be passed from generation to generation."

"So I am a witch but Eva isn't?" Catheryn asked. She tried to politely eat the soup, but after a few bites, she simply gulped it down.

"Seems so," Eva said. "But that would explain why the queen is looking for you."

"Yes," Catheryn said. "She didn't know what I was when she sent me with the pirates, but she found out later. She ordered me to return."

Eva seemed to be mulling this over. Catheryn used the opportunity to ask Eva about her past.

"So where have you been all these years?" she asked. "You were just a little girl when we were separated. How did you survive?"

"I kept thieving, of course," Eva said, matter-of-factly. "What else was I supposed to do? That bastard took you as a slave to pay for what you stole from him, but he didn't give us any money in exchange. I was six years old and had no money and no one to look after me."

Catheryn couldn't keep the tears from falling. She couldn't imagine the hardship little Eva had faced. The things she must have done to survive. "I'm so sorry."

"It's okay," Eva said. "It wasn't your fault. You had no choice but to go with the man. I kept on stealing to survive, but unlike you, I got really good at it." She grinned. "I didn't get caught. I started stealing larger, more expensive things. I got into burglary. Eventually, I found my way into the thieves' guild. I grew up in the ranks, and now I'm a queen, too. Of a different sort."

"You...you're the Queen of Thieves?" Catheryn asked.

Eva's face beamed with pride. "You've heard of me?".

"Not...really," Catheryn said. "Only that there was a Queen of Thieves in NOLA. But as a slave, I didn't know much about what was going on in the city, or the rest of the Division."

"Well, now you know," she said. She then motioned to the people around her. "And these are my loyal 'subjects,' but I call them my friends. My family."

Catheryn wasn't sure how to feel about this. She was glad Eva had managed to survive, but she was disappointed in the path she had chosen. She knew it was wrong to feel so judgmental. How else was the girl supposed to survive? And Catheryn had also turned to thievery many times even after going to live in the Hoodoo House. Eva was clearly proud of the life she had made for herself, so Catheryn would have to learn to accept it.

Catheryn squeezed Eva's arm. "I'm glad you not only survived, but thrived," she said, and meant it. "Is everyone here human?" she asked, looking around.

They all nodded.

"Witches have covens; vampires have clans or crews. We humans have guilds and families," Eva said.

"You're all in danger," Catheryn said.

Eva tilted up her chin, just a little. "I know," she said. "Some of the queen's slaves have escaped during the chaos at her house. We have taken them in. They told us that she has started by slaughtering her own slaves and the vampires who were supposed to turn you over to her. But that is only the beginning of her plan."

"Rainier saw her in a vision, after he drank my blood,"

Catheryn said. "He saw her rounding up all the humans and vampires in NOLA. She called it a cleansing."

"She wants to exterminate all the humans and vampires from the Division," Eve said, confirming Catheryn's visions. "Then she wants to find a way to unite the Divisions and cleanse the entire world."

Catheryn shook her head. "The woman is mad. She must be stopped!"

"I was hoping you would say that," Eva said, smiling. "I could sense you were not exactly proud of me when I said I was the Queen of Thieves…"

"Eva," Catheryn said. "I didn't mean—"

Eva held up her hand. "It's okay, Catheryn. I'm not ashamed, but I know not everyone loves what I do and who I am. But I thought you might be proud to know that I'm also leading the resistance against the Hoodoo Queen."

"What?" Catheryn asked. "There's a resistance?"

"Well not everyone is compliant to just roll over and die," Eva said. "Of course there's a resistance! Not all of humans know the extent of what is happening, but they all know the queen is dangerous. And the few vampires in the area are more than happy to fight back, too."

"And you trust these vampires?" Catheryn asked.

"The vampires need us," Eva said. "And we vastly outnumber them. We haven't worked all the details out yet, but we have a tentative peace treaty in place for now. They are allowed to feed on humans, but not to kill or try to turn any. In exchange we have suspended all hunts on them and let them know which humans are willing to be fed upon."

"That sounds reasonable," Catheryn said. "But what about the witches? The ones who aren't in her coven?"

"We can't trust any of them," Eva said. "The other covens have not been fighting back. We suspect they are allowing her to cleanse the Division of humans and vampires for them and then they will try to overthrow her."

"That's a risky game," Catheryn said. "I think she grows more powerful by the day."

"I agree," Eva said. "You are the only witch we can trust. And from what I have heard, you are the most powerful witch anyone has ever seen. I suppose it's on account of your pure blood."

"So you've heard of me, too?" Catheryn asked.

"Oh, yes," Eva said. "Before Rainier's pirates went to the Hoodoo House, they stopped for drinks in some of the taverns. They told of how you were able to command the sea itself."

Catheryn blushed.

"Is it true?" Eva asked, her eyes sparkling with excitement. "Were you able to control the waves and make them capsize the ship?"

"Not exactly," Catheryn said with a laugh. "There was a storm. I was able to just...nudge it a bit."

Eva laughed. "So modest. But in all seriousness, you need to stop debasing yourself and what you can do. We need you. If you have powers, you need to let them fly. Stop being afraid of yourself."

Catheryn took a deep breath. After all these years, Eva still knew her best. She knew that Catheryn wasn't just holding back out of modesty, but fear.

Eva seemed to sense Catheryn's trepidation. She placed her hand on Catheryn's. "Sister," she said, her eyes watering. "I have waited so long to say that word. I believe in you. You are strong, and you didn't give up on us. It was not a weak child who sold herself into slavery to protect me, but the bravest, most powerful woman I knew, and that was before you found out you were a witch."

Catheryn gripped her sister's hand.

"I know you can help us," Eva continued. "You are probably the only person who can."

Catheryn nodded. She was still scared, but this was what she came here to do. She came here to find her sister and defeat the Hoodoo Queen. Now that the pieces were falling into place, she couldn't back away.

"I'll do it," she said. "*We* will do it. Together."

Eva smiled, and the two embraced. The other thieves cheered and sprang into action, arming themselves with their paltry weapons.

"Wait," Catheryn said. "We can't just go running into the Hoodoo House. The queen is still powerful, especially in her own home." She remembered how the queen even threatened to bring the house down on the vampires if they didn't agree to her terms. "We have to have a plan."

"I agree," Eva said. "Here is what I was thinking..." Eva dragged Catheryn over to a large table where a map of NOLA was laid out. "This is the current layout of the city. We have been drawing in the rising waters. You can see they are practically up the Hoodoo House's front door now."

As a slave, this wasn't something Catheryn had given much thought to over the years, but now, as she looked at the map and the ever-encroaching blue, she realized the city was slowly disappearing.

"What we can do?"

A thieve scout ran into the room. "Miss Eva!"

"What is it?" Eva asked.

"The Hoodoo Queen's coven, they've captured a pirate," he said.

Catheryn's heart dropped. "What pirate?"

"It doesn't matter," Eva said. "She's been capturing lots of pirates. It's part of her cleansing."

"This one is special," the scout said. "It's the one with the bounty on his head."

"Rainier!" Catheryn gasped. "It's Rainier."

"You mean the vampire pirate who took you as his slave?" Eva asked, her eyebrow cocked.

Catheryn blushed. She knew Eva wouldn't understand what Rainier meant to her. *She* wasn't even sure what Rainier meant to her. She had left him, after all. But he was here! That meant he had come for her. He did change his mind; he was the man she thought he was. The man she loved.

She admitted it finally to herself—she was in love with Rainier. She only hoped they would both live long enough for her to tell him.

"He...it's complicated," Catheryn finally said. "He is the reason I found out about my powers. He helped train me so my powers would grow."

Eva nodded thoughtfully. "So you think this pirate is an ally?"

"You said there were other pirates you were working with," Catheryn said defensively.

"Yes," Eva said. "Pirates I have been building relationships with for months, years in some cases. But this is a pirate you just met a few weeks ago when he kidnapped you and drank your blood. Are you sure you can trust him? I don't want to risk the lives of everyone who is putting their trust in me."

Catheryn did her best to tamp down her temper. Of course Eva had a right to be skeptical and cautious.

"I understand your concerns," Catheryn said. "But yes, you can trust him. I would trust him with my life."

"Fine," Eva said. "Then I trust him, too." She spun back toward her fellow thieves. "Get ready, everyone. Looks like we need to rescue a pirate."

CHAPTER 24

"Let me out of here!" Rainier screamed as she shook the bars of his cage.

"Shut it, vampire," one of the witches replied. "No one can hear you down here."

Down here? Rainier wondered. Where was he?

After the witches had attacked him with the black smoke, he passed out. He didn't know where they had brought him, but they had to be acolytes of the Hoodoo Queen. This had to be her doing.

Rainier paced in his cell. Why had the Hoodoo Queen kidnapped him? She wanted Catheryn. That must mean she hadn't found her yet. Catheryn must not have gone to the Hoodoo House as he'd feared. But then, where was she? If the Hoodoo Queen didn't know, that could be why she had kidnapped Rainier, to use him as bait to draw out Catheryn.

It wouldn't work. Catheryn had left him. She had no idea he was here.

Well, she did send the boat back. Maybe she did know the real him after all. Maybe she'd known he would eventually change his mind and come for her. But why hadn't she just wait for him then? Of course, if she hadn't left him, he might not have felt the need to return. He had everything he needed on that island. Without Catheryn there, he had nothing.

Catheryn. That beautiful, impetuous girl. When he found her, he'd have to have a word with her about running off into battle half-cocked. She needed a plan. She needed a partner. What was she doing out there now, all alone? She needed him. He had to find some way to escape and then find his way to her.

He shook the bars to the cell again. They were certainly sturdy enough to keep any human locked up, but for the average vampire, they would be nothing. He would have easily been able to bend the bars when he was at his full strength. But he hadn't been at his full strength since he first drank from Catheryn. He barely had any vampiric strength left in him at all. He could feel that he had some left, but any significant use of it would drain him. But he did have one other trick up his sleeve.

"Hey!" he called out to the guards. "Hey, you!"

One of the guards, a young woman, turned to him, but the other, a woman who looked about middle-aged, slapped her arm. "Don't listen to him!" she said. "Don't look at him. You know what he's capable of."

"What am I capable of?" he asked.

"You can get inside people's minds," the younger one said, not looking at him.

"The Hoodoo Queen can do that, too," he said. "How else would she know I was back in NOLA? Maybe she's in your head right now."

The young woman looked back at Rainier with wide eyes, but then quickly looked away again.

"Stop talking to him," the older one said.

"Come on," Rainier said. "What can I do to you from in here? I just want to have a little chat."

The older one looked at him defiantly. "I know what you're capable of, vampire," she snapped.

Rainier looked deep into her eyes, even from across the room. He emitted a sense of calm over her.

She gasped. "Wha...what is that?" she asked as she took a step toward him.

"Nothing," Rainier said, waving her forward. "Just a little *vampire* magic."

"What's happening?" the younger one asked, slightly panicked. "Should I warn the queen?"

Rainier turned his gaze to her while still keeping the other woman in his thrall. "There's no need for that, lovely."

She smiled and walked toward him. "That...that is nice," she said. "Are you going to feed from me?"

Rainier chuckled but shook his head. "Sorry, not today. Can't drink witch blood." The fact that feeding on Catheryn had gotten him into this sorry state was not lost on him.

"Why does that make me feel sad?" the witch asked.

"Because you know you are missing out on one of life's great pleasures," he said. "Now give me the key."

"Ain't got no key," the older woman said.

"What?" Rainier asked.

"Too dangerous to have you and the key in the same room," she said.

Damnit, Rainier cursed to himself. Well, she was right about that. And the queen was no fool. Of course she would know better than let the guards keep the key in the room. If he commanded one of the witches to go get it, his control would wear off as soon as she left his sight.

"Fine, we will do this the old fashioned way," he said. He lulled the women to come close to his cell, then he gripped both of them by their shirts and banged their heads into the bars. They both fell to the ground, out cold.

Rainier took a deep breath and gripped the bars. He grunted as he used all of his remaining strength to bend them apart, just enough that he could slip through. When he was finished, he almost thought he was going to pass out. His vampire strength was completely gone. He had never felt so weak, not since he was...human. He nearly shuddered at the thought. He couldn't imagine being a weak worthless human.

He couldn't worry about that now, though. He needed to escape. He needed to find Catheryn. He opened the door to the room and slipped up the stairs. When he opened the next door, though, he couldn't believe where he was.

He was in the Hoodoo House.

The damn witch queen had brought him right into her lair. So why wasn't she on his ass already? Surely she knew everything that was going on in her own home. Maybe she was distracted by something. What if she had already captured Catheryn?

Well, he had no way of knowing that unless he got out here. Which he needed to do anyway—this place was too dangerous. He needed to get out and then find Catheryn. Simple, easy, two-part plan.

He walked down a hallway, but the path quickly ended. He hadn't noticed it was a dead end before. He wouldn't have come this way if it was. He could either go left or right, both ways blocked by a door. He went left. After he opened the door, he came to a room that looked like a library. There were now three doors to choose from. He closed the door and decided to go right. When he opened that door, he ended up in the library again.

Rainier groaned and rolled his eyes. *Damn enchanted house!* He took a deep breath to calm himself and then remembered something he had learned about mazes when he was young: always keep your right hand on the right wall. Of course, that probably only worked in human-made mazes, not a living, breathing, hexed house like this. But it was the only plan he had.

He placed his hand on the right wall and walked around the room. He opened the first door he came to and went through. He was at least out of the library. He was back in a long hallway. It was dark, so he couldn't see the end. As he walked, the hallway seemed to keep going. It just kept stretching on and on.

"Come on!" Rainier yelled.

He started running toward the end of the hallway. Finally, he came to another door. Through it, he found a much more mundane room—a kitchen.

Rainier realized he was starving. He grabbed a loaf of bread and found some cured meat and cheese. He ate quickly, hardly savoring a bite. When a door behind him opened, he turned.

"The prisoner's escaped!" she yelled.

Rainier lunged at her, but she dodged out of the way easily. He realized that, along with his vampire strength, his vampire speed was also gone. But at least he still had his natural strength and agility.

Rainier grabbed the witch by her hair. She snatched a knife off the counter and swung at him. He let her go and jumped back. She waved the knife back and forth tauntingly.

"I'm going to enjoy this," she said. "That little bitch is going to get what's coming to her."

"Nathalie!" a voice behind Rainier gasped.

He turned to see another witch had entered the room. He grabbed her and used her as a shield as the one called Nathalie charged at him. Nathalie ran the other witch through. The witch screamed in pain and Nathalie stared in horror at what she had done.

Rainier used Nathalie's shock to get the upper hand. He pushed the injured witch against her, and they both fell to the floor. Rainier then stepped up and punched Nathalie in the face, knocking her out cold. Then Rainier fled the room.

He was now in a part of the house that looked vaguely familiar. He must have been here when he approached the Hoodoo Queen before, back when she traded Catheryn to him. He turned left, then right. Finally, he saw the front door. He sprinted toward it, but five witches stepped in his way. And they were all ready for him. They raised their hands and blasted him with their magic.

Rainier was knocked to the ground, and his breath flew out of him. He gasped for air. One of the witches summoned the black smoke again, using it to pin his arms to his side. Two other witches grabbed him by his arms and led him upstairs.

The second floor was a large open area, and at the far end, the Hoodoo Queen sat on her throne. A large black crow rested on the spine of her chair and cawed.

CHAPTER 25

"We have to go, now!" Catheryn said, anxious.

"Wait," Eva said. "We need a plan. We can't just run up to the queen without a plan."

"But she'll kill him," Catheryn said. "If he fights back and the queen thinks he is more trouble than he is worth, or if too much time passes and she thinks her trap isn't working, she'll just kill him. She'll come after me another way."

"So what?" Eva said. "I know you think this guy is your ally, but what is one less vampire? None of them can really be trusted. He'd be one less thing to worry about in the end."

"Don't say that," Catheryn said. "We have to save him."

Eva frowned, a sadness marring her already roughened features. Catheryn looked around the room and noticed the other thieves were shaking their heads and whispering. She must have seemed like a crazy person.

"Everyone, arm yourselves and get ready to leave," Eva ordered. While they busied themselves, Eva pulled Catheryn aside. "What is going on," she whispered harshly. "What aren't you telling me?"

"Rainier..." Catheryn said. "He and I...it's more than...just friendship."

"Oh my God," Eva said. "You're...in love with a stupid vampire? Are you crazy?"

"Probably," Catheryn said. "I can't explain it. I've tried to deny it. Even when he confessed his love for me, I refused to say it back, but I can't deny my feelings to myself. I love him. I have to help him."

"But...are you sure?" Eva asked. "You know that vampires have the ability to hypnotize you. It's how they get humans to submit to them. They can control witches, too."

Catheryn shook her head. "Not me. He tried. It doesn't work on me."

"Maybe so, but maybe he has some other power over you. He did feed from you, right?"

Catheryn nodded.

"Maybe there is something in the bite," Eva said. "Like a...a virus or something that would make you his thrall."

"I don't think so," Catheryn said. "I hated him for a long time, for kidnapping me, for feeding from me, for the way he let his crew deal with the other slaves. And I know, logically, I should still hate him for all of those things. But I don't. There is another side to him. A kind side, a thoughtful side. He's a good leader and a good man. It's why he's here. I left him on an island. He could have stayed there, out of harm's way. He could have gone anywhere. Another city, another ship. But he's here. He came here for me. He loves me. We love each other."

"I can hardly believe what I am hearing," Eva said. "But...I know what's like when people don't want to accept who you love."

"Really?" Catheryn asked.

Eva nodded and motioned toward a young woman in the back of the room. She had bright blonde hair and shining blue eyes. She was wearing a plain cotton dress and a bloodstained apron. She was helping wrap the wounds of a young man. The tenderness in her touch was easy to see even from across the room.

"She's our medic, or near as we can have one. She doesn't have any formal training, but her mama was a midwife. Her name is Beth." Eva got a wispy look in her eyes as she stared at Beth while she worked. "Not everyone is accepting; we are both so young. But I've more than proven my ability to be a leader so most people keep their mouths shut."

"I...I had no idea," Catheryn said. "You've not even acknowledged her presence since I've arrived."

"Because I have a job to do," Eva said sternly. "I'm the guild leader and can't be distracted. And today I have to lead a rebellion. If I only thought of her, what good would I be? Same for her. She can't save lives if she is worried about mine. We all have a role to play, a job to do. We have to focus, or all could be lost."

"You remind me of Rainier," Catheryn said with a small smile. "He said something similar when he was training me to use a sword. You have to keep your mind on the fight."

"He sounds like a smart man," Eva said. "So he would understand your need to focus on the battle and not him."

It took that for Eva's point to slam into Catheryn. She'd gotten her to agree to the sentiment, but that didn't mean she could agree that Rainier could be forgotten.

"I can't lose him," Catheryn said emphatically.

"I'll do my best to make sure he comes out of this unharmed," Eva said. "But we have to have a plan. Do you trust me?"

Catheryn nodded, but she couldn't help but laugh a bit. It seemed as though their roles had been reversed. Eva was acting like the big sister, taking the lead, giving orders, teaching lessons. They had both grown up to be headstrong and independent women. If they both lived through this, Catheryn imagined they would butt heads many times throughout their lives.

"Okay, so what's your plan?" Catheryn asked.

"Miss Eva," a scout yelled as she came in. "It's starting!"

"What?" Eva asked.

"The cleansing," the scout said. "Several witches were seen rounding people up in the Mardi Gras Coast. They are killing people."

"Everyone!" Eva said. "We knew this day was coming. Troops One and Two, head down to the Mardi Gras and stop the witches. I know they are powerful, but we are numerous. Rally the people behind you. You know what to do!"

"Yes, ma'am," they all called out as they ran out.

"The rest of you, grab the supplies and follow me."

Catheryn, Eva, and the rest of the thieves headed toward the Hoodoo House.

"We need to go to the source," Eva said. "Directly to the queen. If we stop her, all the rest of this madness will come to an end."

"So, your plan?" Catheryn asked. "What is it exactly? I'm listening."

"Oh," Eva said. "I don't have one yet."

"What?" Catheryn had to bite her tongue for a moment and regain her composure before continuing. "All that talk about a plan, and you don't have one?"

"Hey, I was working out the details," Eva said. "This happened sooner than I expected, probably because you and Rainier showed up. The queen probably had to move up her timetable."

"So what are we going to do?" Catheryn asked.

"Let's just see what we are up against first," Eva said.

Catheryn didn't like the sound of that, but she didn't have a better idea, either. They couldn't just sit around thinking while people were being killed.

As they approached the Hoodoo House, they were dismayed to realize they wouldn't be able to get very close. The witches had set up a perimeter around the house. There was a wall with a witch guarding it every few feet. There were several torches set up as well, illuminating the area. If anyone got too close, the witches would see them immediately and strike them down.

"What do you think?" Eva asked.

Catheryn shook her head. "I'm not sure. We can't take them out one at a time because that would give them time to regroup and focus their efforts."

"Can you take out many at once?" Eva asked.

"I...I don't know," Catheryn pressed her hands against her face, trying to summon some sense of calm. "I've never tried, and I don't want to practice now. If I mess up, it would be over."

"We have gunpowder, lots of it," Eva said. "But if we just use fire to set it off, it could take too long to ignite, giving the witches a chance to stop it or escape and regroup. If we set it up around the parameter, could you ignite it all at once?"

Catheryn nodded. "I think I can."

Eva explained the plan to her people, who quickly sprang into action. Catheryn was awed by Eva's ability to so easily direct her followers. She was an excellent leader.

Eva returned to Catheryn's side. "It will just be a moment," Eva said. "Are you ready?"

Catheryn was nervous, but she nodded anyway. "Yes," she said. "I'm ready."

Eva placed a reassuring hand on Catheryn's arm. "Everything will be fine, you'll see."

Catheryn had her doubts, but she had to remain positive, hopeful. If she doubted in their abilities, then she already lost. She had to believe they had a chance. She had to believe *she* had a chance. Nothing else mattered. Even if Eva's people were able to stop the cleansing, even if she was able to get Catheryn through the Hoodoo House's defenses, it would be up to Catheryn to stop the Hoodoo Queen. No one else was strong enough. No one else had pure hoodoo blood. In the end, it was all on Catheryn.

And she was terrified.

Eva shook Catheryn's shoulder. "It's time," she said.

Catheryn followed her and took her place far enough away from the wall, but close enough that she could see all the powder kegs. She took a deep breath and called upon the fire in her soul. Her hands ignited in flame. She threw the fireballs at the kegs, and all at once, they exploded, taking out the wall and half a dozen witches.

"Attack!" Eva yelled, drawing her sword and pistol.

The other thieves raised their weapons and their voices as well. Together, Catheryn, Eva, and the thieves charged the Hoodoo House.

The witches were in shock. Many were killed in the initial attack, and several more were injured in the yard. For the witches still in the house, they seemed unsure what was happening. Some threw open the windows to the upper floors, but the thieves were able to easily shoot them. Some witches came from around the side of the building, but they were shocked at the scene they saw, so the thieves had the upper hand, usually able to land the first blow. Some of the witches were able to regain their senses and fight back, but not in the numbers they needed.

Catheryn had only one goal in mind—getting through the front door.

As she ran, a witch came up on her left side, but Catheryn shot her with a blast of energy, knocking her away. Two witches came up on her right, but again, Catheryn took them out easily. These witches had been training for their entire lives and had been taught by the Hoodoo Queen herself, but they were no match for Catheryn.

The world blurred around her as she reached the porch. She flew up the steps. Nothing could stop her now.

Well, except for maybe one thing...

The Hoodoo Queen herself.

CHAPTER 26

"Rainier," the queen purred from her throne. "So nice to see you again."

Rainier stared the Hoodoo Queen down. "Too bad I can't say the same of you," he said through gritted teeth.

"Because you've lost," she said. "This time you will not be able to steal from me or threaten me. From where I am sitting, this is a very nice meeting indeed. Please, join me as my guest."

She motioned for the other witches to let him go. Those around him dissipated. This was hardly an act of friendship, though, but one of boasting. She knew he wasn't a threat to her, even if he wasn't restrained. She was trying to humiliate him by showing just how weak his position was.

"You won't win," he said, refusing to give into her intimidation tactics. "Even if you kill me, your plan will fail."

"What plan is that?" she asked innocently.

"This genocide of everyone except witches," he said.

"Oh, darn," she said. "You figured me out. Well, no matter. It's too late. The cleansing has already begun."

She reached behind her chair and pulled out a severed head. She tossed it at Rainier's feet. It was the former second mate of his ship. He must have taken over as leader after Mathis was killed and he jumped ship.

"So you killed them all, even after you promised to make a deal with them?" Rainier asked.

"I promised them clemency *if* they brought me Catheryn," the queen said. "When they returned empty handed, what good were they to me?"

Actually, he had to agree with the queen there. They were fools for returning to NOLA without Catheryn. He probably would have done the same thing in her position.

"You and I are not so different, are we?" the queen asked, as if she could read his thoughts. "You are also ruthless, aren't you? You don't grow from a scrawny stowaway to the most powerful vampire pirate captain of the dark seas without slitting some throats."

Rainier didn't respond. He didn't know how she knew so much about his past, but he wouldn't give her the satisfaction of acknowledging just how right she was.

"Like me, you also believe in the dominance of your species," she continued. "You don't just accept your life as a vampire, you relish it. You believe that vampires are the superior race and should be the only race, if only you didn't need humans to survive. But given the chance, you'd slaughter all witches and enslave the humans, wouldn't you?"

"No," he said, though even he doubted the truth of his words. "Maybe at one time, but not now. Not anymore."

"Not since you met Catheryn, you mean." The witch cackled. "You are a fool, you know that. A vampire falling in love with a witch."

Her laughter increased to an almost manic frenzy. The other witches in the room joined in.

"It was probably not one of my better choices," Rainier said with a shrug. "But it is what it is."

He tried to act like it was no big deal, as though Catheryn was nothing more than another conquest. He didn't want the queen to use him as a weapon against her.

The queen laughed again. "So macho. What a *man* you are, pretending not to care. It doesn't matter if you love her or not. She loves you, and she will come for you."

"I don't think she does," Rainier said. "I'm sure you know she left me on that island to die."

"Yet you stand before me," the queen said. "Stop posturing. It doesn't become you."

"So what now?" Rainier asked.

"Now," she said, "NOLA has a worthwhile future for the first time in centuries. Soon, the city will be rid of the human and vampire vermin. Then Catheryn will come for you, and I will convince her to join me. Together, she and I will be the strongest coven in the NOLA Division, and one day, the world."

"Catheryn will never join you," Rainier said. "She's not evil. She doesn't even want the powers she has."

"She will join me," the queen said. "I will show her all of life's possibilities. Teach her the true potential of her powers."

"And you don't think she will use them against you?" Rainier asked. "She's not like you. She won't join your cause. She will fight you."

"Then she will die," the queen said. "It is no matter to me. Even if she does have pure hoodoo blood, I am still stronger, more experienced. I will defeat her. She will join me or die."

Rainier sighed again and looked around the room. He tried to pretend that all this witch business was of no concern to him, but inside, he was panicking. He had to get out of here. He needed to find Catheryn and help her. She couldn't do this alone.

On one side of the room was a fireplace with a mantle. On top of the mantle was a sword. He knew that going for the sword was probably a poor choice. With only human strength and speed, she would probably stop him. But what other choice did he have? He couldn't just stand here and do nothing.

He elbowed the witch standing next to him in the face and then lunged for the sword. He grabbed it and spun around, slicing through a witch that had tried to attack from behind.

As he advanced toward the queen, she stood up from her seat and grabbed a nearby staff. He attacked, but she easily deflected him to the left, the right.

"*Nyang'anya silaha,*" she said, causing the sword to fly from Rainier's hand. Then she grabbed him around the throat.

He gripped her wrist, but he couldn't force her to let him go. Her strength was incredible. Even if he'd still had his vampire strength, he wasn't sure he'd have been able to stop her.

"You are a fool, Rainier Dulocke," he said, raising him off the ground. Rainier felt his eyes grow big as his feet began to lift from the floor. "Vampires and witches cannot love each other. A vampire cannot defeat a witch. You might be able to kill one of two of us, but you cannot win over all of us. We are the more powerful species. We are the true heirs of the Rift. We are the ones who will rise from the ashes and create a new world, a new age."

She placed her other hand on his chest, and he began to feel the little life force he had left drain from him. He struggled to breathe, for his feet to find the ground, to get away. But he was only flailing. There was nothing he could do. She was killing him. She wasn't even interested in using him to find Catheryn anymore. She would kill him now.

He would never see Catheryn again.

CHAPTER 27

Three witches ran at Catheryn. She shot one with fire, dodged the other, and called upon a strong wind to lift the third up into the air and then bring him crashing back down. Eva ran up behind Catheryn and quickly stabbed the one Catheryn had evaded.

"Where was she keeping Rainier?" Catheryn asked.

"The scout said he was in the basement," Eva replied as she shot another witch that was charging toward them.

"Then let's go!" Catheryn said.

She remembered the basement, back where this all began. She had been hiding in the closet, first from the witch she had injured in the kitchen, then from the pirates, when the back of the closet gave way and she fell at Rainier's feet. That one moment had changed her life, and she would never be the same.

There were so many witches. They never seemed to stop coming. Catheryn didn't remember seeing this many witches in the house when she lived there. Witches were the least populous of all the races. She remembered Eva saying something about the other witch covens refusing to join the rebellion against the queen. Some of them must have joined with her to help support her evil plan after all.

Even though Catheryn could fight with a sword, thanks to Rainier, it didn't come naturally to her. Hoodoo magic was coursing through her veins, and she wielded it like a musical conductor's baton. She only had to hold out her hand, and the world was at her command. Fire seemed to come easiest to her, shooting from her fingers effortlessly. In larger, more open spaces, she could also call forth a wind. She was unable to call forth water, however. She had to be in the presence of water to control it.

As they ran from room to room, Catheryn was able to quickly take out some of the targets, but Eva had her back, easily picking off anyone that Catheryn missed.

They ran down the stairs and into the dungeon, but it was empty, except for two witches lying on the floor. The bars of the cell were bent, creating a hole large enough for a man to get through.

"He's gone!" Catheryn cried.

Eva waved her hand at the bent bars. "He must have escaped."

"But where could he be? Where would he have gone?"

"I don't know," Eva said, pulling her back up the stairs. "It doesn't matter. He probably went looking for you. He's probably safe. Don't worry about him. We should go find the queen."

Catheryn was annoyed, but Eva was right. They were here to both rescue Rainier and take out the queen. Rainier hadn't just been removed from the cell, he had escaped. He was probably long gone. Once he found out that Catheryn was part of the assault on the house, maybe he would come back and fight along with the rest of the resistance. Whatever he decided to do, they would find each other later, then they would sort everything out. Then they could plan their future together.

But for now, Catheryn needed to face the Hoodoo Queen.

She still doubted she would be strong enough to take the

woman down. She had a strength and wisdom of age that Catheryn did not possess. Her natural abilities surely could not trump untold years of study and training.

But Catheryn did have Eva by her side. Eva was strong, agile, and brutal. As the witches came at them, Eva sliced their throats, took them out at the knees, and even pinned some to the walls of the Hoodoo House with her daggers. She fought with a cold efficiency that Catheryn couldn't help but admire and fear.

From outside, Catheryn could hear the other thieves fighting the witches. Eva had also said they had some vampires on their side. They were working as a team for the survival of all. Together, maybe, just maybe, they could win.

"The queen is probably in her throne room," Catheryn told Eva.

"And where is that?" Eva asked.

"Upstairs," she replied.

Eva laughed. "Of course it is in the opposite direction. Oh well. Let's go!"

Together, Catheryn and Eva fought their way back up to the main floor. Just as Catheryn started up the stairs to the next floor, she heard Eva scream. She spun back around. A witch had Eva in her clutches. Eva's face was twisted in pain, and blood was dripping from her side.

"No!" Catheryn screamed.

She ran over and shot the witch with fire, throwing the witch across the room. Then she shot the witch again, and again. The fire pouring from her fingers seemed to be coming from deep within her soul. It didn't even matter if the continued assault was needed. She was fueled by pure anger.

"I only just got her back," Catheryn declared. "You'll not take her from me again!"

The witch was long burned to a crisp, but Catheryn couldn't stop until she felt Eva's hand on her shoulder.

"Catheryn," Eva said.

Catheryn turned to her sister and held her tightly. "I'm sorry. I don't know what came over me."

"It's all right," Eva said. "I'll be okay."

But Catheryn knew Eva was lying. She was holding her side, blood seeping through her fingers.

"But you're injured," Catheryn said, tears filling her eyes.

"This little thing?" Eva said. "Just a flesh wound. I've had worse than this. Don't let me stop you, you hear me? You have a job to do. Get up there and stop the Hoodoo Queen."

Catheryn hesitated. Not because she was afraid of the Hoodoo Queen, but because she didn't want to leave her sister.

"If you die," Catheryn said, "I'll never forgive you." The two girls pressed their foreheads together and Catheryn squeezed her sister's face.

"Same goes for you," Eva said.

Catheryn finally forced herself to let her sister go. Eva limped toward the front door. Beth would be somewhere behind the line, tending to the injured. If anyone could save Eva, it would be her.

Catheryn took one last long look at her sister and then headed up the stairs.

There before her, across the long room, the queen was holding Rainier by the throat, inches above the ground, his feet flailing, gasping for air. The queen's other hand was on his chest. A golden glow was flowing from Rainier into the Hoodoo Queen.

She was draining his life force.

"Stop!" Catheryn yelled. "Release him! I'm the one you want."

Surprisingly, the queen did exactly that. She let Rainier fall to the floor, as limp as a ragdoll, and he crumpled at her feet.

CHAPTER 28

Rainier couldn't move. Even when the queen dropped him and he felt the sharp pain from hitting the floor, it was as if his body had been completely drained of energy. He was alive, but he could not move. He simply laid there, lifeless on the floor. He could only watch as Catheryn faced the Hoodoo Queen alone.

"Catheryn," the Hoodoo Queen cooed with her arms outstretched. "My child. You came back to me."

Catheryn took a step back. "I am *not* your child," she spat. "What have you done to Rainier?"

"He doesn't matter," the queen replied. "All that matters is that you have returned, and now, together, we can cleanse this city and create a haven for all witches."

"I'll never join you," Catheryn said. "Witch, vampire, human, all people deserve to live."

The queen bristled. "The humans are weak and the vampires are competition. It is simply the law of nature, of evolution. We are the next step in the progress of the species. No longer human, we have long risen above that. And finally we have grown in strength and numbers to take our rightful place on earth."

Rainier saw Catheryn pause. Was she actually considering the queen's words? She couldn't. She must be forming a plan. Rainier tried to call out to her, but only raspy air came out.

Catheryn took a step toward the queen. "You are evil," she said. "And I will stop you."

The queen shrugged. "That's too bad," she said. "I had hoped to have you by my side. But believe it or not, Catheryn, I don't need you."

"Why are you really doing this?" Catheryn asked, narrowing her eyes.

"What do you mean?" the queen asked. "I already told you why."

"No you didn't," Catheryn said. "You know a witch can be born of two humans. You know two witches can create a human. It's an impossible task. So why?"

Before the queen could answer, one of her acolytes charged at Catheryn, but Catheryn calmly pointed at a stool and sent it flying across the room, smashing against the witch's head and sending her to the ground.

"You might be unique," the queen said. "But hardly necessary to the survival of the witches."

Another witch ran toward Catheryn. Catheryn raised her hand, causing the rug to fly out from under the witch's feet. The rug then rolled up around the witch, suffocating her.

"Pure blood hoodoo witches had been dying out since Africa," the queen said. "Yet hoodoo witchcraft remained. It thrived, even. Look at me. No one is stronger than I am."

Catheryn took a step toward the queen. "Except for me. And I will stop you."

The queen laughed. "I have been watching your progress. It is impressive for someone not raised to hone her magical skills, but believe me, you are still a pale shadow of what you could be if you joined me."

Catheryn took a deep breath. "I guess there is only one way to find out."

At that, she called forth a strong gust of wind. It filled the room, swirling around everyone, including the Hoodoo Queen. The wind tightened around the queen, forming what looked like a tornado around her. It got smaller and tighter. Rainier wasn't sure what Catheryn was doing, but he thought maybe she was trying to crush the witch with the power of the vortex.

The queen let out a laugh that was low and heavy. "Is that the best you can do?" she asked. She raised her arms, breaking the vortex and sending a blast of wind through the room, knocking everyone back.

Everyone except Catheryn. Her feet stayed planted to the floor.

"Very good," the queen replied with a toothy smile. "You think quickly. That is a good trait for a witch to have."

Then she caused one of the boards in the wall to break loose and fly toward Catheryn like a stake. Catheryn dodged. Then two more stakes flew at her. Catheryn jumped to avoid them. Then five stakes came at her. She grabbed a silver serving platter off a nearby table and used it as a shield. She then threw the platter like a Frisbee toward the queen, hitting her in the shoulder.

The queen gasped and gripped her injured arm. She glared at Catheryn. Apparently, she truly hadn't thought Catheryn stood a chance, that she would even get a shot in.

"You underestimated me," Catheryn said. "But that has always been the case. You never saw me for who I was or who I could be. I was nothing to you."

Catheryn took a step forward. A vase flew across the room and smashed against the side of the queen's face. She didn't even see it coming. Catheryn didn't even have to use her hands or say a word to use her powers anymore. Blood trickled down the side of the queen's face.

"That is why you must be stopped," Catheryn said. "Human,

witch, or vampire, we all have the potential for greatness. Yes, some people can be terrible and do awful things, but that doesn't depend on their race. Witches can be evil or good. Humans can be strong and vampires can love."

"It's not about goodness, or love," the queen spat. "It's about survival. Only one race can survive."

Catheryn shook her head. "We will never agree on this."

"Then you will die!" the queen screamed as she shot a ray of powerful light at Catheryn.

Catheryn formed a sphere of darkness in front of her that absorbed the queen's power. Then Catheryn was able to turn that power back on the queen, shooting her across the room.

Rainier was in awe of Catheryn. She walked toward the queen without fear. Any insecurity about her powers or who she was or what she could do was gone. She had risen above herself and nearly floated as she walked. Her hair and clothes fluttered in the turbulent wind that still filled the room. To Rainier, she looked like a magnificent goddess.

The queen became enraged. "I might have underestimated you before," she said. "But I won't make that mistake again."

She lifted her arms, and wisps of smoke flew around the room. It looked as though the wisps had faces—terrible, horrifying, distorted faces with red eyes and pointed teeth. Many were misshapen like gargoyles but they seemed human. They let out cackling laughter as they surrounded Catheryn.

"You have the blood of your ancestors to give you power," the queen said. "Well, I have special *friends* as well."

One of the ghastly creatures smacked into Catheryn's head. Another flew through her chest, causing her to gasp.

Catheryn used light attacks on the creatures, but they had no effect. She then tried darkness, and then wind, but the creatures didn't even shudder. None of her attacks worked. She didn't know what the wisps were or where they came from, so she didn't know how to fight them.

"I am the Queen of Hoodoo!" the queen said as she stepped toward Catheryn. "You cannot stop me! I have the power of a thousand dark souls!"

The demons were overwhelming Catheryn. Rainier felt his heart beat rapidly in his chest, but he could barely move. He could do nothing but lie there and watch Catheryn, the only woman he had ever truly loved, die.

Catheryn stumbled and fell back next to Rainier. She wasn't looking at him, but was staring in fear at the queen as she approached.

Rainier mustered the last of his strength and moved his hand, barely touching Catheryn's. If they were going to die, at least they were going to die together. Catheryn felt his touch and looked at him. Their eyes locked. Catheryn's eye welled with tears, but she tried to give him a reassuring smile.

"I'm sorry," she said. "You never should have followed me back here."

"There is nowhere else I'd rather be," he said with a dry raspy voice, "than at your side. I love you, Catheryn."

"And I love you," she said. "I admit it! I...I love you," she repeated.

Her chest rose and fell as she took several deep breaths. Her eyes widened as though she was remembering something. She turned back to the queen. She forced herself to her feet.

"You might have millions of wicked souls giving you power, but I do have one thing you don't," Catheryn said.

"And what's that?" the queen asked.

"The love of a vampire." With that, Catheryn held out her hands, and fire spewed from them with the blazing heat of a thousand suns.

The Hoodoo Queen screamed and called to her minions. They rushed to her, surrounding her, trying to protect her from the fire, but they were instantly burned and disappeared. The queen's horrifying screams filled the house, but soon were quieted as she turned into ash.

The queen was dead, but there was no time to rest. The house was burning. Catheryn tried to summon a harsh enough wind to extinguish the flames, but she appeared exhausted, and the light breeze only made the fire worse. It would probably take time before she could summon an element again.

Instead, she ran to Rainier's side. "Can you walk?" she asked him. "We need to get out of here."

Rainier tried with all his might to move his legs, but he couldn't. "Just go," he said. "You need to leave. I won't make it out of here. I'll just hold you behind. We'll both die."

"I'm not leaving without you," Catheryn warned through her tears.

Catheryn took a deep breath, summoning power from deep inside her, and she picked Rainier up. Slowly but surely, she carried Rainier out of the Hoodoo Queen's throne room and down the stairs.

The few witches that were left were also fleeing the house like rats, but outside, Eva's thieves were waiting for them.

Catheryn stepped through the door of the burning house, and everyone gasped as though surprised she had survived. Catheryn stepped down from the porch and collapsed to her knees in the yard. She placed Rainier gently on the ground.

"Eva!" Catheryn yelled. "Beth! Help me!"

A dark haired woman who must have been Catheryn's sister limped toward them, followed by a willowy blonde.

"You...you found her?" Rainier asked.

Catheryn nodded and held his hand tightly. "I did. I found my sister."

Beth held a cup of water to Rainier's mouth. He tried to drink, but he was so weak his head just fell back.

"Rainier," Catheryn cried. "Stay with me!"

"I'm sorry, Catheryn," he said.

"Beth!" she yelled "Do something!"

Beth shook her head. "I...I don't see any wounds. What can I do? I can't see what to heal."

"Catheryn," Rainier said softly. "Catheryn, don't be afraid."

"I don't want to...*can't* go on without you," Catheryn said. "I need you. You give me strength. You give me power. I wouldn't be a witch without you."

"You were always a witch," Rainier said. "I just helped you find her hiding within you. But you are on your own now. I know you can do it."

"Rainier..." She shook her head, cradling him as tears slid down her face and dropped from her chin "Rainier, don't you dare leave me."

Rainier raised his hand and touched her cheek. "Human or vampire, it wouldn't matter if I could just stay here with you."

"Then stay with me! Stay..." she cried.

Rainier thought he heard her say something else, but the world faded to black.

CHAPTER 29

The Hoodoo House continued to burn. People cheered. The Hoodoo Queen was dead, and the people no longer had to live in fear of her. From the slave quarters behind the house, the slaves and vampires that had not yet been killed poured out, grateful to be alive. There was much celebrating. But in the midst of it all, Catheryn's heart was broken.

She was weeping deep heaving sobs that couldn't be staunched.

"Rainier! Rainier!" she cried as she held his limp body in her arms.

Eva wrapped her arms around her sister and held her. She didn't speak, because no words would bring her sister comfort.

Catheryn felt weak and empty. Without Rainier, she didn't think she could ever call forth her hoodoo power again. Inside the house, when the queen had almost defeated her, it was her love for Rainier that gave her the strength to succeed. She realized there was no more powerful force on earth than love.

Legend said that the love of a witch and a vampire had shattered the world, causing the Divisions as they were today. Catheryn now believed it. Her love for Rainier was not earth shattering, but it had given her the strength to defeat the Hoodoo Queen. If Rainier had lived, who knew just how strong she could get.

Catheryn was mourning Rainier, but she was also mourning for herself, for whatever within her that was dying with him. Finally, Catheryn could cry no more. Her tears were spent. She continued to hold Rainier, unable to let him go.

"Catheryn," Eva finally said. "We should leave this place. The smoke is choking the air. And you need to rest."

"I can't," Catheryn said. "I can't leave him!"

"You don't have to leave him," Eva said. "Love can last, even beyond the grave. You are exhausted now, but you are still Catheryn, a pure blood hoodoo witch. You can recover."

Catheryn only shook her head.

"I know it hurts," Eva said. "He was a good man. If there was anything any of us could have done to save him, we would have, even if he was a vampire."

"Where will we go?" Catheryn asked. "I can't leave him."

Eva rubbed her sister's arm. "I understand," she said, waving some of her men over. "We can bring him with us, back to the guild house. He'll get a proper burial. I promise you."

Catheryn nodded. She tried to stand, but she was weak, all of her energy spent on the battle and on grieving for Rainier. Beth ran over and let Catheryn lean on her. Catheryn let the men pick Rainier up, but she held his hand as they walked back to the guild house.

As they walked the streets of NOLA, word of what Catheryn had done seemed to travel faster than they did. People—human, witch, and vampire—lined the avenues and cheered as Catheryn passed.

But Catheryn could not enjoy her moment as hero of the city. Her thoughts were only of Rainier, and she couldn't imagine a way forward without him.

Back at the guild house, the men laid Rainier on a table. Catheryn sat by his side and held his hand.

"Take all the time you need," Eva said. "When you are ready, we can have his body prepared for burial."

Eva took her leave. The city was celebrating for now, but the cleanup and rebuilding work would need to start soon, so Eva headed out to assess the damage.

Catheryn stroked Rainier's face. Out of the corner of her eye, she noticed Beth was watching them. Her eyes were wide, and she was biting her lower lip.

"What is it?" Catheryn asked. "You look like you want to say something."

Beth stepped closer and laid her delicate fingers on Rainier's wrist. "I...I'm sure it's nothing," she said. "I don't know anything about vampire physiology. But...but I can't help but wonder..."

"Wonder what?" Catheryn asked.

"How do you know when a vampire is truly dead?" she asked. "Other than staking them through the heart or cutting off the head, how do you know? They don't breathe or have a pulse like humans, not exactly anyway."

"What are you saying?" Catheryn asked. "Are you suggesting he is still alive?"

Beth paused, choosing her words carefully. "I don't want to give you false hope. But I have heard that vampires, when they don't have blood for long periods of time, they go into a torpor state, like hibernation, but it is very much like death. A frozen, waiting state."

Catheryn nodded. She had heard this before as well.

"What happened to him?" Beth asked. She had not been in the house, had not seen what the Hoodoo Queen did to him.

"The Hoodoo Queen," Catheryn explained. "She was draining his life force from him."

"But you stopped her?" Beth asked. "You interrupted the... ritual, or whatever she was doing?"

Catheryn nodded.

"So what if he isn't dead, but his body has slipped into a torpor state. To protect him, preserve him," Beth said.

Catheryn stood up, her heart beating with excitement. "So what do we do?"

"Give him blood would be my guess," Beth said.

"What blood?" Catheryn asked. "Human or witch?"

"He was feeding on you on the ship, right?" Beth asked. "Why not yours?"

"I don't know," Catheryn said. "My blood was sustaining his life, but it was draining him of his vampirism. That's why he was too weak to fight the queen. He was very nearly human."

"Strange," Beth said. "I've never heard of that effect of witch blood on a vampire before. Maybe it is because of your hoodoo blood."

"Whatever the cause, what if it caused more damage instead of bringing him back?" Catheryn asked.

"But his death was not caused by a lack of human blood," Beth reasoned. "It was caused by magic. Magic is in your blood. If I was a gambling woman, I would bet that blood infused with magic would have a better chance of restoring him than boring old human blood."

"What's this talk about human blood?" Eva asked, walking back into the room.

"Beth thinks that Rainier might just be in torpor. That my hoodoo blood might be able to bring him back," Catheryn said.

"That's my woman," Eva said. "Beauty and brains. So what are you waiting for?"

"I...I don't know," Catheryn said. "I really don't think it will work. But I have hope. If I try and fail, that hope will be dashed."

Eva pulled a dagger from her belt and handed it to Catheryn. "Hang on to that hope, sister."

Catheryn held her breath as she took the dagger. She pricked her finger and then held it over Rainier's mouth. One, two, three drops fell.

"Is it enough?" Catheryn asked. "Should I try more?"

"Just wait," Beth said. "We can try by increments. No need to drain you dry just yet."

They waited for what seemed like an eternity, but was probably only a few seconds.

Rainier gasped.

CHAPTER 30

R*ainier...*

Rainier heard the most beautiful voice saying his name. He thought it must have been calling him to whatever afterlife was waiting for him. He couldn't see anything, but he had the sense he was floating. It reminded him of the night he and Catheryn were sitting in the life raft together, the night she agreed to be his devotee. The night his world changed...

Rainier...

He knew that voice. He would recognize it anywhere.

"Catheryn," he tried to call back to her, but he could barely speak. His sweet beautiful Catheryn. His powerful goddess. God, how he loved that woman. What he wouldn't give for just one more day with her.

"Rainier!"

He heard it more clearly that time, like she was standing right next to him. He tried to turn his head, look left and right, but all was black.

"Catheryn," he called out, a little more clearly that time. He thought he felt a little stronger, like there was more to him than just his mind floating in space.

He was falling. He was no longer suspended in the black, but something was happening. He could feel the wind on his face. The light. He could see light.

He gasped as his eyes flew open.

"Rainier!" Catheryn cried as she held him tight.

"Catheryn," he said as he took in his first full breath. "You're choking me, girl!"

"Oh!" Catheryn let go, but she still gripped his shoulders and looked at him, fear and wonder in her eyes. "Are you...are you really here? Really alive?"

"I...I don't know," Rainier said as he touched his arms, his stomach, his legs. "What happened?"

"Beth figured it out," Catheryn said, gesturing toward the blonde woman he had seen earlier. "She knew about torpor and said that since your death was caused by magic that maybe magic could bring you back." Catheryn was rambling without taking a breath.

"Who is Beth?" Rainier asked. He looked around the room. He saw the woman who was probably Eva, but there were several other people around as well, all rather scruffy-looking humans. "And where am I?"

"Oh," Catheryn said. "Right. This is Eva, and Beth is her girlfriend and a medic for the thieves' guild."

"Thieves' guild?" Rainier asked.

Catheryn nodded. "Eva is their queen...of sorts."

"You're the Queen of Thieves?" Rainier asked, impressed.

"You've heard of me?" Eva sked.

"Not by name, but reputation," he said. "So, Beth knows about magic? Is she a witch?"

"Oh, I don't know about magic," Beth said, humbly. "I just thought that since magic killed you, magic might bring you back."

"It was my blood," Catheryn said. "My blood saved you."

"My hero," he said. He reached up and pulled her in for a kiss.

She tasted sweet. She finally pulled away, a sheepish grin on her face, most likely embarrassed to be so affectionate in front of the others.

"But there is one caveat," Catheryn said. "I think you might be human now."

Rainier held his hand to his chest. He felt his heart beating. Even though he still had a heartbeat as a vampire, it was weak, faint, barely discernable. Now, his heart was beating strong and clear, like a human.

"Your heartbeat is normal and your color is returning," Beth said. "I'm sure you will feel strange at first, even weak. But eventually you will get used to a new normal."

"I'm human..." Rainier said. He could hardly believe it. "So...mortal?"

"I have no idea how old you are," Beth said. "But you appear to be in your late twenties. So, yes, you are probably mortal, but I expect you to still live the rest of a normal human lifespan, another forty or fifty years. Maybe more. But be careful, because you can be killed much easier, just like any of us."

Rainier let her words sink in. Human? What would that even be like? He had thought of humans as nothing more than food for as long as he could remember. Now he was one of them? He took a deep breath.

Catheryn squeezed his hand nervously. "Are you...okay?" she asked. "I know you are probably disappointed."

Rainier kissed her again. "How could I be disappointed knowing I get to wake up to that face every morning for fifty years?"

Catheryn laughed, but a few tears fell from her eyes. "I thought I'd lost you," she said. "I didn't know how I was going to go on."

"Well, now you don't need to worry," he said.

"We have other things to worry about," Eva said.

Catheryn turned to her. "What do you mean?"

"The city is in chaos," she said. "The death of the queen has created a power vacuum. Many people are celebrating, but the leaders of the various clans, covens, and guilds are already plotting. If we don't act quickly, someone else could take over, someone worse than the Hoodoo Queen."

"Who could be worse than the Hoodoo Queen?" Catheryn asked.

"I don't want to find out," Eva said.

Rainier sat up straighter. "So what do we do?"

"Catheryn needs to go out into the city, make an appearance. Use her powers to start rebuilding. She is the city's savior. She needs to let the people know she won't abandon them."

"I...I don't know what to do," Catheryn said. "I'm not a leader. You know more about leading people than I do. You are already a queen. You should seize power while you have the chance."

Eva shook her head. "I'm a leader of a small faction of humans, nothing more. If I wanted to lead the city, I'd have to do it by force. You, though. You could inspire the people. They could rally behind you. They would choose to follow you."

"I...I don't think I can..." Catheryn blushed and looked away, as if embarrassed by the attention.

Rainier took her hand. "I know you can."

"You have always believed in me," she said. "When no one else did, even me. The only reason I am even a witch is because of you."

"No, that's not the only reason. But now, it's time to believe in yourself. Time to become a queen."

She blushed again, but this time she didn't look away.

"You're right," she said. "I mean, I saved you, didn't I? Then I can save this city, too."

Rainier hopped off the table, and he, Eva, Beth, and the rest of the thieves followed Catheryn outside.

The city was indeed in ruin, as Eva had said. Many of the shops had been looted and ransacked. Fire had razed part of the city. There were dead people and vampires strewn about. People were fighting.

Catheryn, with help from Eva and Rainier, took charge. As she walked through the city, anyone who was fighting she used chains of smoke to bind them. She used pillars of ice to keep damaged building from falling. She called up a wave from the sea to wash the streets clean.

And the people—human, witch, and vampire—followed her.

When she arrived at the port, she stood on a stack of crates and addressed the people.

"We will rebuild," she said. "And everyone—human, witch, and vampire—will find safety in the NOLA Division."

The crowd cheered, but some of the people had concerns.

"The vampires are monsters!" one man called out.

"The humans only want to hunt us down," a witch cried.

"What are we to eat?" a vampire asked.

"I know it will be difficult at first," Catheryn said. "But we will find a way. Together, we will learn how the three races can co-exist. But it will take time. Have faith in me, and we will find our way through the storm together. Trust me, I've guided through worse!"

The people cheered again. They believed in her, trusted her.

"Three cheers for Queen Catheryn!" someone called out.

Slowly but surely, the whole crowd joined in calling for Catheryn as their queen.

Catheryn bowed to the people, acknowledging her acceptance of the title. That sent the crowd into a near frenzy of joy and excitement.

Rainier helped Catheryn down off the crates.

"Eva," she said. "I need your help."

"I know," Eva said. "I'll take care of it. My people will work on establishing order through the city and act as an emergency police force. But it will only be temporary. You'll need to appoint a council with members from every race to advise you on how to move forward."

"Hold on," Catheryn said. "For my first act as queen, I want to appoint the queen's official consort." She gave Rainier a sly smile. "Will you accept? Will you marry me and be my king?"

Rainier laughed. "I will!"

They kissed, and the crowd cheered again.

When Catheryn and Rainier separated, they couldn't stop smiling. Finally, Catheryn turned to Eva. "Okay," she said. "Now you may rally your temporary police force to establish order."

"Aye-aye, ma'am," Eva said, giving her new queen a salute and running off to do her bidding.

"There are still many concerns," Rainier said. "The waters are rising. There is a food shortage, for humans and vampires. The world is still fractured."

Catheryn nodded. "I know. I have no doubt that my rule will be plagued with problems, some too large for me to fix. But we will take it one day at a time."

They linked their fingers and walked back toward the guild house.

"But what about you?" Catheryn asked. "Can you really live as a human? I know you loved your life on the sea."

"I don't imagine I will stay landlocked forever," Rainier said. "If you can establish peace in the city, who knows, maybe that peace will extend to the ocean as well. One day I will return to the water, with you by my side as my pirate queen."

"And you, as my hoodoo king," Catheryn replied.

The two embraced, never to be parted again.

The End

~

Read more books from the Berkano Vampire Collection at
www.fallensorcery.com

Get a free book from Leigh Anderson when you subscribe to her
Newsletter today!

Get two free books from Rebecca Hamilton when you subscribe
to her Newsletter!

ABOUT LEIGH ANDERSON

Leigh Anderson has lived in Asia for many years, which inspires her to write romances set in ancient China. Her friends and family have no idea what she writes in the dark hours of the night, when sleep eludes her. She keeps her fantasies safe within the confines of her writing….for now.

Visit her Website
Subscribe to Leigh's Newsletter

ABOUT REBECCA HAMILTON

NEW YORK TIMES, USA TODAY, AND WALL STREET JOURNAL bestselling author Rebecca Hamilton lives in Georgia with her husband and four kids, all of whom inspire her writing. Somewhere in between using magic to disappear booboos and sorcery to heal emotional wounds, she takes to her fictional worlds to see what perilous situations her characters will find themselves in next. Represented by Rossano Trentin of TZLA, Rebecca has been published internationally, in three languages.

Visit her Website
Subscribe to Rebecca's Newsletter